Some connections are carried by the tide.

Sea Glass

LORI JOSEPH

Some connections are carried by the tide.

Sea Glass

LORI JOSEPH

This is a work of fiction. All characters, places, and events portrayed in this novel are either products of the author's imagination, coincidental, or are used fictitiously.

Imprint: Independently published

Library of Congress Control Number: 2026941165

Sea Glass
ISBN 9798994979501

PREFACE

The story of Sea Glass was written to celebrate the mystery of how inanimate objects capture our attention. They speak to us and find their way into our pockets, our homes, and our hearts.

We hold onto these treasures, and for whatever reason, they fill us with hope or evoke something quite memorable. They are a glimpse into our cognitive behavior and connect us to our past. Inherent or not, sometimes we need a talisman to hold onto when we follow our intuition and believe in the unknown.

—Lori Joseph

EPIGRAPH

When someone or something is important to you, they strike a chord and touch your soul. Interdependence has its own rhythm, inviting us to dance, to discover everyday miracles. There's no denying their energy exists. Those particles are cast into the universe and forever change the world as we know it. Pocketed from the coast of Maine and brought to America's Heartland, a wish gets fulfilled. —Sea Glass

1

SEA GLASS

It is late September. There's a pot of vegetable soup in a rolling boil on the stove, and the salty tang in the rising steam reminds me of tumbling in the ocean. Lost in thought and heartbroken, Sophie is at the sink with suds up to her elbows. The house is quieter now that the kids have moved on with their lives, and Eric, Sophie's husband, is consumed with his work. We've been living on the plains for several years, and I can't remember the last time Sophie held or touched me.

There are streams of water running down the window from the condensation in the room. Water runs down Sophie's face, too. The dog usually follows her around, but today, he lies on the kitchen floor, occasionally lifting an eyebrow and waiting for her next move. We all remain silent and motionless. The soup pops, startling us and causing the dog to jump up off the floor to sniff. I feel the cool water pool around me on this windowsill. My porous texture soaks it up, and before I know it, my luster is being restored. I'm gleaming all over, waiting for her to notice me any second.

Wiping the tears from her face onto her shoulder, she opens her eyes and reaches for me. I am clenched between her prune-like, sudsy hands in the darkness, feeling her despair. Being someone's touchstone, a talisman, is a beautiful gift. I am honored she found and chose me to journey with her family. Without Sophie, I wouldn't have had the opportunity to move around the country and watch the kids grow up. I have been illuminated by sunlight and moonlight, included in decorative displays on their tables, and carried in a tote on trips for good luck. I even got to go to the hospital when Will, Sophie's son, needed sutures. She really held me tight then. The sweat from her palms was nearly as salty as the ocean. I have a few areas that are forever smoothed, like a scar. The phone rings, and the dog and I perk up. Sofie sets me down and quickly dries her hands. She turns the soup down low and takes the call.

Looking around, I discover I'm no longer on the window's ledge but next to a bunch of empty jelly jars on the counter. I hear Sophie confirm our address while she is on the phone. She says she'll be ready at 8 a.m. on Thursday. Every time we've moved, I've been wrapped in tissue and tucked away, unsure of where I'm going and whether or not I'll be rediscovered.

When we moved to Nebraska, it took nearly a year for her to find me, and to be honest, I think it was by accident. Sophie was looking for *Love Poems* by Pablo Neruda, a little book with a soft pink cover and gold print. I enjoyed his writing very much and was content with resting on his words. The box I was packed and stored in was dropped. That's when I slid from my tissue wrapping onto page twenty-seven of his book. It was rather peculiar that the poem was titled *Absence.*

Eventually, I was found and placed on her windowsill above the kitchen sink. I've been sitting here for a very long time, watching and waiting. Outside, the winds were often so violent that Sophie rarely opened the window for fresh air. When she did, I found myself covered with grit that was blowing across the plains.

The cat jumps up on the counter and drinks from the faucet by placing her paw under it to collect the drips, closing her eyes to lick the water from her paw. It seems she only does this when no one is home. She uses her water bowl on the floor when the family is there. I don't know how Sophie packs the cat whenever we move, but here I am in this jar with the lid screwed tight, waiting for my next destination.

Three days have passed, and now there's a sea of boxes in the room. The look on Sophie's face is resolute. All alone, she is all business today. There are no tears. The cat senses change and sulks around the boxes, leaving her food untouched. Sophie picks me up and places me in a box with a couple of pot lids, a pie pan, some candlesticks, and a champagne flute, and we head to the car. I'm hoping we go back to the ocean.

Sophie found me there many years ago when the family vacationed on the waterfront. Combing the beaches daily with her children, they collected shells, stones, and trinkets. The tide was going out when she spied me lying next to a piece of driftwood. Sophie held me to the sunlight, examining the slight trace of red veins in my turquoise color. The kids took turns holding me in their little wrinkled, wet, sandy fingers. I was fascinated by them too! Will let Isla, his little sister, place me in the window of a sand castle, and then he used me as an eye for the sand lizard they created. It was a great day to experience new things and be a part of their family. I was thrilled when they took me home with them.

Now, we are on the move. Sophie put Pence the dog and the crated cat in the back seat, then placed my box in the back of her car. It's very dark in here. After a short drive, the vehicle comes to a stop. She pops the hatch open and gives the box containing me inside the faceted jelly jar to a stranger, takes a receipt, and drives away.

The woman lifts me from the box to examine me, and then carries me to a white metal shelf where I am left next to a flawed glass vase on one side and a trivet bearing the words "Smoky Mountains" on the other.

I have been sitting on this shelf for a few months. Sophie gave no good-bye, no nothing. I've been abandoned.

*The afternoon sun drifts over the tumbleweed surf
ducks and geese become buoys floating the wild blue
signaling with honking fog horns, as if we might crash.
Their wings swell with motion while I remain eddied—
my ocean, landlocked.*

2

SOPHIE

Sophie takes a final walk around the yard to look at the perennial garden she attempted to create, despite the frequent hailstorms in Nebraska. She plucks one lone rose, remembering the day they purchased the home. She thought it was unusual for the real estate agent to inform her at the closing that, "many couples don't survive the move to this town." The agent had no idea their marriage had already endured several relocations. Sophie pushes the trash to the curb, deciding there is no need to go inside the hollow shell that had once been their home.

With her belongings packed into her Toyota 4Runner and the compact rental trailer, she heads east, taking the family pets with her. The estimated drive time to Dublin, NH, is one day and five hours, covering 1,894 miles. Although she has experienced many moves, she's startled by the wave of emotions she feels when the Howard Jones song, *No One Is to Blame,* comes on the radio. The lyrics cut right through her as she thought of her own hopes and dreams going down the drain. She alternates between changing stations and shutting the radio off to ride in silence. Driving is easier during daylight hours, when she can view the countryside to distract herself.

Driving through hours of darkness only amplifies her disbelief. Her body revolts when she recalls the day her suspicions were confirmed. By happenstance, Sophie found a feather earmarking a page in a book containing a handwritten love letter to Eric.

Fortunately, her best friend, Liddy, has offered her a place to stay until she gets this situation with Eric sorted out and gets back on her feet. As lifelong friends, Liddy and Sophie call each other weekly to keep in touch. So it pains Sophie not to be utterly truthful with Liddy, especially since she is offering her refuge.

As she drives into the night, Sophie recalls that summers were especially beautiful in New England when they lived there. The warm days were rarely humid, and their family preferred to stay close to home, enjoying outdoor activities with a network of families who lived in Dublin. Occasionally, their family ventured to the ocean for an overnight stay. Eric was never fond of going to the beach, but conceded when outnumbered.

One summer, they were fortunate to spend an extended weekend in Ogunquit, Maine. According to legend, the Abenaki Indians named the area Ogunquit, meaning "beautiful place by the sea". Will and Isla, their children, were happy, curious, and content to hang out at the beach. Time there felt effortless and free.

Perkins Cove was the perfect place to picnic and explore tide pools. They walked along the ocean to town on the Marginal Trail to get ice cream. On their walk back to the cove, Sophie felt overwhelmed; a premonition pulled her to explore an inlet just ahead. The tide was receding, so they scrambled down the rocks to look for treasures. They watched hermit crabs scurry across the sand. They searched and found several shells, and a starfish when Sophie caught a glimpse of something next to the driftwood. She dug into the wet sand to find a beautiful piece of turquoise-colored sea glass. Beyond thrilled, finding the sea glass was like winning a lottery jackpot.

They stretched the day out as long as possible before leaving for home. As the kids packed their shells in a bucket, Sophie tucked the sea glass into her pocket. She couldn't risk losing it when it brought her such joy.

From then on—when it wasn't in her pocket for good luck—she displayed it with their collected treasures on a small tray in the living room to remember their trip. Over time, their collection grew, marking memories of trips to the mountains, lakes, and rivers.

Sophie remembers staring out the window to where a sycamore tree once stood on their property in Dublin. She and Eric enjoyed sitting on the double swing under the gigantic tree. Will and Isla, along with the neighborhood kids, also enjoyed playing on the swing.

Sophie is a registered nurse, but when they decided to have children, she and Eric thought it would be best for her to stay at home to raise them. At the time, her choice was in stark contrast to the popular career-focused women's movement sweeping across the country. Having earned her degree, Sophie felt like she had a foot in both camps.

Eric was a salesman, and his territory was in New England. They lived frugally, and when a better-paying position in a new territory became available, they moved. In fact, Eric had already made three career moves before their family moved to New Hampshire.

After nine years, a flurry of mergers and acquisitions led to rapid buyouts and sales. Eric saw the writing on the wall, and they headed west for his new job. Although it was tough for the family to make these moves, Sophie and

Eric always made it an adventure for the kids, assuring them that they would make new friends and create new experiences.

As for Sea Glass, Sophie was happy to keep it with them as it continued to be her good luck charm. She liked to take it along when she searched for a specific item or needed help finding the perfect gift. Sometimes, she just felt the need to keep it in sight, like on the windowsill above the kitchen sink.

One year, Eric's signing bonus was used to purchase a second home in Vero Beach, FL. When the kids left for college, Sophie became a snowbird spending the coldest months in Florida's warm, sunny climate. Eric stayed with her for a week or so each month. They were accustomed to living apart, as his career often took him away for extended periods. Before, when he returned, she attributed his moodiness to reacclimating to family life on top of the stress at work, or that she was somehow failing as a spouse. Sophie began to simmer. She felt like the fool who'd been played.

Stopping to take a break and walk the pets, she slammed the car door shut and cried out, "Damn that real estate agent, he was right. After twenty-five years of marriage, all the moves, and now this!"

Breathing in the late-night air afforded Sophie the composure to resume her drive. After several more hours on the road, she shifted, readjusting her seat. She began speaking aloud to her angels and guides, asking for compassion and understanding — asking God to guide and protect her on this journey. The stars were a reminder that she was not alone in her travels.

Sophie plowed through the snacks on her passenger seat by eating one potato chip, one licorice, or one grape for every five miles she drove. Emotionally eating her way east.

She remembered her father telling her that she needed to start pushing back from the table a little sooner than later. He constantly evaluated someone's weight and had no filter when sharing his opinion. It was embarrassing for Sophie to witness this firsthand. When she confronted him, telling him that not all people can be a particular shape or size to meet his standards, he replied, "I'm just telling it like it is." Sophie met her eyes in the rear view mirror and realized at that moment that her frankness, which Eric despised, came from her father.

Finally, the drive is behind her, and Sophie sees Liddy waiting on the porch to greet her. After a long hug, she immediately offers to help Sophie by taking the pets for a walk in the backyard and giving them fresh water and food.

"You must be exhausted," Liddy says. "Would you like something to eat, or would you prefer to stretch out on the bed?"

Sophie sighed. "I'd like to take a hot shower and stretch out if that's okay."

Liddy shows her to the bedroom she has prepared and sets the towels in the bathroom. "Take as much time as you need. I've got some errands to run. There's plenty of food in the fridge, so please help yourself."

"Thank you, Liddy. I can't imagine what I would've done."

Fatigued, Sophie never budged from the bed until the next day. The sun was well up when she made her way downstairs.

"It's good to see you, girlfriend. Would you like to have some lunch? I was about to make a sandwich."

"That sounds great." Sophie replied, rubbing her stomach, realizing how hungry she truly was.

The grilled cheese sandwich never tasted so comforting to Sophie as it did at that moment. This was the beginning of her new reality. She takes in her surroundings and notices that Liddy's environment is unchanged. She has the same decor and dishes from when Sophie and Eric lived in Dublin. In comparison to her own life, it's surreal to consider the differences. They eat the sandwiches and reminisce about the days their families got together for game nights, when nostalgia brings Sophie to tears.

"I never wanted to become a statistic, Liddy."

"Sophie, you will find your way through this. I did it, and so can you. Just take it one day at a time."

And that was what Sophie did. Living with an old friend, searching for work, and facing the unknown were major adjustments. To avoid dwelling on the past, Sophie eventually enrolled in a Reiki class and found part-time office jobs to occupy her days. Her nursing days were so long ago that obtaining a nursing position now required her to return to school for two more years. And that was something she wasn't interested in doing.

She found solace in taking walks and helping Liddy in the vegetable and flower gardens. On weekends, Liddy taught pottery classes at the local artisan's club, and Sophie would often go along. She found it therapeutic to immerse her hands in the clay.

One night, after her students left, Liddy noticed a thoughtful Sophie standing at the sink. "What's on your mind?"

Sophie shakes her head. "I don't know where to begin," she says as she finishes drying the dishes.

Liddy wants to comfort her. Instead, she quietly leaves the room.

3

SOPHIE

They divorced based on irreconcilable differences. Neither of them could make the other feel valued. Eric, the product of a loving yet unstable mother, struggles to understand women. He accused Sophie of being defensive or acting like an ostrich with her head in the sand. Never realizing he was fueling her low self-esteem, it was the very reason Sophie began to distance herself from Eric. She developed this coping skill as a child when her parents fought with each other or her older siblings. Nothing was ever rationally discussed between them, which she believes contributed to her inability to communicate effectively.

After years of presenting Sophie with beautifully wrapped gifts and never receiving the response he expected, Eric grew weary. It was their seventeenth anniversary before Sophie realized she was incapable of truly appreciating such kind gestures. Sophie saw the beautiful gift wrap as a waste of money. As for the gifts, before she met Eric, the only gifts she had ever received were practical, useful items. No one had ever gifted her something of beauty for the sake of joy. Sophie never considered herself deserving of such love. Although vulnerable, she felt safe in opening up to Eric. After all, it was their anniversary. When she shared this epiphany with him, his response was, "It's okay, I'm used to it," succinctly ending their conversation. From this exchange, Sophie finally understood his attraction to extremely effervescent personalities; they give him the attention and emotional support he thrives on. An elixir, if you will.

Over time, they drifted further apart, finding it more challenging to have a conversation with one another. Fortunately, Will and Isla were away at college, so they didn't have to endure the final years of their parents' marital turmoil.

To make matters worse, before their divorce was finalized, both of Eric's parents passed away. While on his way home from settling their estate, he received notification that due to corporate restructuring, his position was eliminated. Shattered, Eric left Nebraska to move into their Florida home. Taking the beautiful vase passed down to him from his maternal grandmother. It was the only keepsake that he deemed necessary to take and left Sophie to finalize the disbursement of everything else.

4

WILLA

Unlike most days in Sidney, Nebraska, the wind lay back that afternoon, making nine-year-old Willa's entrance into the Goodwill store a little easier. She always wondered if it was okay for her to look and shop here since both of her parents worked. She knew these stores were meant to help furnish homes and provide clothing for families who experienced hard times or tragedies like fires or tornadoes. To avoid embarrassment, she looks around to see if the coast is clear before she slips into the store.

A bell hangs on a tattered string, striking the glass door, announcing her entrance and that of every visitor. She rationalizes her visits of curiosity with the knowledge that her mother regularly makes donations at the store's back door after routinely clearing space in the closets or cupboards. It was always her Mom, never her Dad, as he could never part with anything.

Once in a while, Willa comes upon a familiar item in the store and tries to remember where she'd seen it before and from whose house. For instance, she recognizes the squirrel salt and pepper shakers and knows they once sat on her grandmother's table.

Like a museum to her, the store boasts a collection of wares from ordinary people. When she's in a creative mood, Willa loves to go there for what she calls Inspiration Runs. The original wooden floor is gritty as always, and two fluorescent lights flicker over the women's sequined tops. In the background, a 1950s radio plays the daily Hog Report and Swap Shop, a program where folks try to make a few dollars on unwanted goods by pitching a sale "On Air."

The aisles are narrow, with floor-to-ceiling metal shelves the length of the store. Willa makes her way to the back of the store and discovers a fancy-cut glass jar. There's something inside that she's never seen before. Willa unscrews the lid and holds it in her hand to inspect its smooth, worn finish. She holds it to the light, and its beautiful turquoise color becomes brighter.

She turns towards the front of the store, holding the piece up, to find the clerk staring at her.

Willa asks, "Can you please tell me what this is?"

The clerk takes it from Willa's hand, examines it, and says, "Sea glass."

"Sea glass?"

"Yes, it's from the ocean," the clerk tells her, plucking the piece from her and putting it back into the jar before handing it to her. Willa screws the lid on tight, gripping the possibility. Nothing has ever felt more certain in her nine years than purchasing this treasure from the sea. The jar is too big to fit in her coat pocket, so she carries it home with both hands, stopping at every other telephone pole to gaze at the sea glass. The wind picks up again and pushes at her back along the Lodge Pole Trail to home.

Opening the front door, the scent of cooked bacon lingers in the air from the BL's (BLTs without the tomato) they had eaten earlier. Willa's Mom found it challenging to find a good, ripe tomato in town, so she stopped trying. Her mother was spoiled by the heirloom beefsteak tomatoes her own mother once grew. Those tomatoes were as big as Willa's face and didn't need a sprinkle of sugar. Willa remembers it took two hands to carry them when she picked them from the garden, and a large dinner plate to serve them on once her grandmother sliced them up.

In addition to having a green thumb, Willa always looked forward to eating her Grandmother's sugar cookies. When Grandpa was alive, he'd play his harmonica for Willa. His false teeth would slip and challenge him, but he still tapped his toe and played his best, inserting a few breathless lyrics to the song.

Willa takes the jar to her bedroom to study her purchase. Holding the sea glass in her hands feels so rare and full of magic. She considers its color and origin as she surveys the world map covering the wall. Closing her eyes, she dreams.

5

SEA GLASS

Willa is fearless. She needs me way more than Sophie ever did. I am Willa's talisman; we go everywhere together. I absorb her feelings and give her hope. It doesn't matter that I don't have a voice. I am the best listener, and she leans on me for comfort. Late at night, when she lies in bed crying, whispering her thoughts, I can feel her emotions. Her salty tears have brought us even closer together.

I had no idea the roller coaster I'd be on when she found me at the Goodwill store all those years ago.

When she was about to leave for college, Willa's mother asked, "How did you get to be so strong?"

It is incredible to me that she even had to ask.

Before she graduated from high school, Willa faced the loss of several important people in her life, all from cancer—her best friend, her trigonometry teacher, her favorite uncle, a neighbor, and her father—which created a massive void within her that she never mentioned.

Maybe that's why her big brother, somewhere around the age of sixteen, developed an addiction. Maybe he chose to numb himself from the pain of loss. His first taste of alcohol came when he worked for a restaurant at the local golf course, and the staff would help themselves to leftover wine or unfinished drinks. Sometimes, the older waitstaff would slip him a shot or two of liquor instead of sharing their tips. In time, his addiction grew with the number of cars he totaled. Willa's parents took measures to get help for him, but nothing ever worked. Certain there would be another phone call from the police, she grew up accepting his behavior and death as part of her reality.

Did I mention Willa was in two major accidents; one from bicycling at the age of ten and the other from skiing at the age of fifteen, suffering concussions from both? The first one left her unconscious in the middle of a macadam road. She thought she heard a car coming from behind and looked over her shoulder to check, and didn't see the huge pothole in front of her. She flipped over the handlebars and hit the road face-first. A neighbor traveling the road found Willa and took her to the hospital. Willa's face was covered with cinders, and her eyes were swollen shut. The doctors were unable to determine if any cinders were embedded in her eyes at the time. Fortunately, there were no broken bones. Willa's parents brought her home to recover on the sofa where they could keep a close watch.

Willa lay there hearing her mother recount the accident to family and friends on the telephone, telling them she looked like a monster and that the men who were in the emergency room from a motorcycle accident couldn't believe Willa looked worse than they did. After several days, the swelling went down, and she was able to open her bloodshot eyes. Miraculously, Willa was able to see, and there were no scars, only a tiny cinder that remains under her right eyebrow.

The second concussion came from a reckless skier who crossed over the tips of Willa's skis while on a school trip, or that's the last thing she can remember. It wasn't until the following morning, when Willa woke up in a state of panic and nausea, that her parents realized that something was wrong. Willa didn't remember returning her rental skis or that her father picked her up at the school to take her home. Once her parents did some inquiring with the ski group, they discovered what had happened on the slope the night before, but no one from the group knew that Willa was really hurt. Another trip to the hospital revealed Willa suffered a whiplash and concussion.

When Willa traveled with the National Honor Society to Disney World, the clique in high school thought it would be a good idea to bully her, telling her she dressed like a slut. The thing is, Willa's mother purchased the outfits for her to wear on the trip. She never told her mother what the girls said or how badly she felt since her mom was already dealing with her alcoholic brother and her dad's cancer. The same girls spread a rumor in school that she was pregnant with an upperclassman's child after they saw him kiss her while on a ski trip.

What must a young girl do to overcome such awful heartache? How does she process pain when it presents itself as a part of life she must accept? I wonder. Certainly, she is not alone, as many people experience trauma and hardships, but what does it do to a person when they never give voice to those emotions? It makes me wonder about my own existence and what I've learned from Sophie. Willa is much younger than Sophie, but there's an underlying thread connecting these women. They've been conditioned to always keep their chin up for the sake of appearance.

6

SEA GLASS

Unlike most of her classmates who would be attending universities and colleges throughout the state, Willa planed to study visual communications at the local community college—until she received an unexpected letter from Graham Burkes' Law Office: *Dear Ms. Jessop, Our office represents the estate of Eva M. Lloyd. Please see the enclosed DEED made on the 5th day of June 2007 by and between Eva M Lloyd, hereinafter referred to as Grantor, and Willa M. Jessop, hereinafter referred to as Grantee, for the conveyance of a remainder interest, and the reservation of a life estate....*

The news of this inheritance came as a huge surprise to Willa. She was a toddler when her great-aunt came to Nebraska once for a visit. Beyond that, there was no correspondence, not even a card, during the holidays. Had it not been for a single faded photograph of Eva holding Willa, she would have no recollection of ever meeting her. Willa's mother said, "Eva was an only child. She was a school teacher, never married, and didn't have any children."

Willa is stunned that Eva willed her cottage and its contents to her. According to the deed, the property is in Maine. She immediately searches the internet for 37 Derringer Road in York County, Maine, to find that the property is in the town of Ogunquit. The world suddenly opened its doors for Willa. After carrying me around all of these years and sharing her ups and downs, I'd almost lost hope that we would ever leave this landlocked town. But today is different; Willa's eyes teared with excitement and wonderment, just like the day she found me. We began to imagine, to dream. The thrill of setting out on her own far outweighed the sadness of leaving Sidney and her family for both of us.

7

SOPHIE

Sophie contemplates where and how she fits in as she drives around the lake with the windows down. The fresh scent of pine softens her core, and she pulls over to take in the view of Mount Monadnock from the shoreline. The lake's surface reflects the cerulean sky and the mountain peak. Sitting on a bed of pine straw, she begins sobbing, releasing her anger and heartache. "Dear God, give me strength and peace. Be with all of us affected by divorce."

Feeling completely spent, she drifts off in the warmth of the sun.

After some time, she is startled awake by the call of a vigilant crow sitting on a branch, maybe ten steps from her. Its stark black body is backlit by the setting sun. As it flies off, the branch springs, reminding Sophie of her own resilience. She stands to stretch, taking a deep breath, and notices the lump or tightness in her throat from earlier is gone. Feeling grateful, she inhales several more times deeply, connecting with the earth's energy.

Sophie fondly recalls a visit with Mim, a woman with lots of wisdom and moxie whom she met years ago. Mim was a well-respected "go-to" for her tireless orchestration of acts of kindness throughout their community.

When Sophie invited Mim for tea, she had no idea Mim was in search of someone to handle correspondence for fundraisers and to write articles to submit to the local news to promote upcoming events. They sat at the dining room table when Mim noticed a stack of journals on the sideboard. She motioned to them and asked, "Who's the writer?"

Sophie shifted in her seat while spooning some honey into her cup and replied, "Oh, I'm not a writer, I just enjoy jotting down some memories and little stories that come to me. Once in a while, I take a crack at a poem."

"By the size of the stack over there, I'd say you're a writer," Mim quipped. "Have you submitted anything to be published?"

Mim's interest in her writing piqued a little curiosity in Sophie. She set her spoon down and got up to retrieve one of the journals.

"No, I don't have anything published, but this morning I came across some poems that I wrote a while back. I honestly didn't think they were too bad." Sophie replied with a self-deprecating tone.

Exceptional at reading people, Mim asked, "May I read one of your poems?"

"Sure, I guess." Sophie opened to a page in the journal and handed it to her to read.

She was surprised to see Mim, an educated, strong woman, tear up after reading the poem. Mim told her the poem took her back to a time when she was a little girl. A time she had all but forgotten. Sophie recognized Mim's discomfort with the memory and quickly changed the subject by offering Mim a cookie to go with her tea.

"Thank you for sharing your poetry with me," Mim said as she wiped away the tears. "You are a wordsmith. Is there any chance I can recruit you to volunteer your talent for some community correspondence?"

Pleased that her words meant something to Mim, Sophie agreed to lend a hand, which led to writing a variety of letters and a monthly newsletter with an occasional poem included. Being a wife and mother are definitely rewarding for Sophie, but she feels an additional sense of purpose or fulfillment to help Mim and their community.

They'd enjoyed a good visit when Mim matter-of-factly said as she stood to leave, "When I die, I'd like the epitaph on my tombstone to read, *She did what she could.*"

Relating to Mim's request, Sophie picked up a flat stone and launched it. She watched as it skipped seven times across the surface of the lake, leaving the stone and her burdens to sink into its depths.

8

SOPHIE

There are fourteen messages on the answering machine when Sophie arrives back at Liddy's home. The first thirteen are from Eric's number, with no message, just a silent void after the beep while he waited for her to answer. On the last call, he finally left a message."Sophie, pick up. I know you're staying with Liddy. I just want to talk with you and I thought, well, I'm here and I would like to know how you're doing. Please call me."

Without missing a beat, Liddy pours each of them a glass of wine.

"He's got no right to ask how I'm doing." Sophie downs the wine as if it were water. "He should've thought about that a long time ago."

"Sophie, do you think he wants you back?"

"I don't care. Isn't it ironic that Eric calls today? I am not ready to speak to that liar. Today, for the first time in months, I can finally feel my lungs."

Liddy winces when she hears the word liar, but not knowing the full story, she says, topping off Sophie's glass, "Nightcap?"

"Liddy, I have put everyone else's needs before my own for so long. I don't regret my time with my children, but I gave up my nursing career and my membership to the Writers Guild. I remember having no fear or reservations about sharing my writing. I was thrilled to put words to paper and write for the joy of it. Stories I've heard from strangers often inspire my writing. It's as if they know they can depend on me to listen.

"You know, there were times I felt like a freak magnet because of the unusual and bizarre things people have shared with me. My family was uncomfortable when they witnessed these exchanges. For whatever reason, I was never afraid of these people, and I thought if they cared enough to share their story with me, they must really need to talk with someone. Do you remember when Will was hesitant to go to the store with me because he didn't like it when those individuals approached us? As an adolescent, he didn't have the patience to stand and listen to them. He still jokes about me having a tattoo on my forehead or a sign on my back that says, *I'll Listen.*

Liddy sets her wine glass down. "You know as well as I do, people can pick up on one another's energy. People are drawn to you because you emit the energy they need. Will takes after you. Like it or not, eventually he's going to discover he is a lot like you. Especially when they start approaching him to share their stories. Sophie, you have a gift, and just because you didn't pursue a nursing career doesn't mean you're no longer a caring person. You did the right thing by taking care of your children, and now it's time to take care of yourself."

"Thank you, Liddy. Sometimes, I fall into self-doubt and find it difficult to pull myself out of the rut."

"I understand, and it's okay for you to have those feelings so long as you don't make it a habit to wallow in unpleasant thoughts. I'm turning in. I've got an early start tomorrow. "Oh, by the way, a letter came for you. I set it on the dining room table. Don't forget! Good night."

"Sleep well," Sophie replies as her gaze moves to the table, noticing the envelope for the first time.

9

SOPHIE

After taking Pence for a walk, Sophie grabs the letter on her way to bed. The return address on the envelope is for the artist colony, where she applied for a job. Unsure whether to open the letter, she weighs the possibility of rejection or acceptance. After her emotionally charged day, the thought of being denied is so unbearable that she throws the letter onto the desk.

Tossing and turning well into the night, she has to know if she got the job. She gets up, turns on the lamp, props the pillows up, and crawls back into bed with the cat to open the letter.

Dear Sophie,

We are pleased to offer you the Administrative position at The McGrady Artist Colony.

You indicated you were interested in a full-time job. Since the position is only part-time, we would like you to chair our community writers workshops, enabling us to accommodate your need for a full-time position.

Please sign the enclosed acceptance letter and return it by April 7th. Once we receive your acceptance, we'll set up an introduction to go over the details.

Welcome Aboard!
C. B. Sutherland, Interim Administrator

A sign from above, she thinks as she settles back under the covers, assured now of a few good hours of rest.

10

WILLA

The town of Ogunquit is picture-perfect this morning. A forest green wooden shingle with the name Graham Burkes Law Office in gold lettering hangs on the outside of a refurbished eighteenth-century home. On either side of the door are large paned windows and planters filled with a gorgeous array of flowers. The aroma from the bakery across the street adds to its charm. Willa notices that the air is crisp, layered with an unfamiliar scent of saltwater, and her anticipation grows.

As she steps in front of the law office, she imagines how her Aunt Eva must have felt signing over her property. Taking a deep breath, she opens the door and is greeted.

"Good morning. May I help you?" says the woman behind the desk, *Carol*, according to the desk plaque.

"Yes, Carol, I'm Willa Jessop. My aunt, Eva Lloyd, is, I mean, was, a client of yours. She left me her home here in Ogunquit. I was hoping I could finalize the paperwork and pick up the keys."

"Mr. Burkes is out of the office for a meeting this morning. Let me check to see if Tilghman, his associate, has time to see you. Have a seat, Ms. Jessop."

Stepping from behind her desk, Carol looks out the window.

"Oh… is that your car parked out front?" She disparagingly asks, as if it weren't obvious. There was no one else waiting in the office.

Sheepishly, Willa nods, knowing it's pretty evident, loaded with boxes, blankets, pillows, and empty wrappers on the front seat.

Adjusting her denim shirt and combing her fingers through her curly hair, she waits for Carol to return from behind the closed door.

Willa scans the room, taking in the numerous community service awards and plaques received by the Burkes Law Office. There is a framed magazine article with a photograph of Mr. Graham Burkes and Tilghman on a golf course. The headline reads, *Prodigy Son Returns*. Although Mr. Burkes is bald, both men are very handsome with a star-quality smile. Willa notices Tilghman has a head of thick black hair and a strong, slender build.

"Tilghman will be right out, Ms. Jessop."

"You must be Willa," Tilghman approaches with a hearty handshake. His smile puts her at ease.

"Yes, nice to meet you." Willa's relieved he has time to see her without a scheduled appointment. "Come on in, and let's wrap things up. Do you have your ID?"

"Is a driver's license good?"

"Yes. That's perfect."

Willa pulls her license from her pocket, and Sea Glass drops onto the floor in front of Carol, who continues to assess her. Willa quickly grabs it and tucks it back into her pocket.

"You can leave your license with Carol so she can make a copy of it for the files. Your Aunt Eva was a great lady. Unfortunately, she retired before I attended Witmore, but she taught several of my clients, and they speak highly of her. Tell me, what are your plans for the property?" Tilghman opens the top right desk drawer to locate the keys.

"Well, this is my first time seeing the ocean. I thought I would live there while I attend community college." Willa replies.

"Wait, are you telling me you've never seen her place?" Tilghman asks with surprise.

"I am. In fact, the only photo I have of Eva is when she held me as a baby when she visited Nebraska." Willa said, shifting forward in her chair with an eager look of anticipation on her face.

"That's amazing. I'm sure you'll have a great time exploring the area. I just need you to sign this document acknowledging you're in receipt of the keys. The new deed has already been filed with the town clerk," he says, stamping the signed document to make it official. "Don't forget to pick up your license from Carol on your way out," said Tilghman, checking his watch."Ms. Jessop?"

Willa turns to see he's opening the door for her.

"Welcome to Ogunquit!" he says, adding to Willa's excitement.

When she leaves the attorney's office, a waft of freshly baked bread lures her across the street.

"So," Carol's eyes are fixed on Tilghman, "how long do you think that Flatlander, I mean Ms. Jessop, will last before she sells?"

Tilghman watches Willa cross the street and go into the bakery."Carol, you have got to be kinder to folks moving here. Remember, you were not born here either."

"Hmpf, you know as well as I do that every time a newbie comes to town, it changes the community," she remarks. "They move here and want what they left behind. They show up at town meetings demanding change. If people would stay away, we wouldn't see our taxes constantly increase. I've lived here since I was two, and now I can barely afford the taxes to keep my home. Mark my words, newcomers are pushing us locals out."

He turns to look directly at Carol. "Rest assured, I don't think Ms. Jessop is going to be building a mansion next to you, or cause your taxes to increase. She's enrolled at the community college if that tells you anything."

11

WILLA

Willa feels alive when she steps into the bakery. Its pulse, a vibrant contrast to the coffee shops she stopped at on her way to Maine. People are chatting about the weekend events as bakers are bringing trays of fresh buns and cookies to the counter. Coffee beans are being ground while Ella Fitzgerald songs play in the background. A preschool group is gathered in a reading area set up with a pint-size table just for them to enjoy their mini-muffins.

While waiting for her order, she notices a long line of mugs hanging above the counter where the regulars can grab their favorite. In front of the bakery, there's a long table surrounded by retirees, each with a unique coffee mug. All of this energy adds to her excitement to check out her new home, just ten minutes away.

As she turns onto the side street, she rolls the windows down to hear seagulls calling. She's on sensory overload with all of the newness. Nearly every home along this narrow road has a boat in its side yard or driveway. The homes are more like cottages, lacking front yards. She drives as far as she can go when the road takes a sharp right turn. The route now parallels the ocean with sand dunes and sea grass blocking her view of the water. All of the houses are on her right with a distance between them. Some homes are weathered more than others and blend into the landscape. There are vibrant beach roses marking the entrance to each driveway, dusted with sand.

Only a few more to go before she runs out of road. As she searches for number thirty-seven, the road ends in a cul-de-sac where a cluster of mailboxes stand for the remaining homes perched on the crest. Aunt Eva's cedar mailbox is the second from the left. Willa drives up the corresponding lane to discover her new home.

A gray two-story cedar shake house with deep blue shutters sits atop the crest. Willa parks and sprints to the other side of the house to find it sits right on the oceanfront. She kicks off her shoes, already filled with sand, and runs to the water. The forceful sound and rhythm of the waves give her pause. Willa compares the area to the openness of the plains. This gift, this vast expanse of sky and water, is something she's dreamed of seeing ever since she found me.

Willa pulls me from her pocket and promptly dunks me into the ocean. It is exhilarating. The cold temperature of the sea shocks her and triggers so many memories for me. Long ago, when I was in the ocean, I learned so much by watching people. Some would use the day to walk, talk, and play in the water, while others would sit silently under their umbrellas, barely exchanging a glance, let alone words. I was captivated to see families return year after year and witness their stories unfold.

12

WILLA

As Willa turns to flee from the encroaching tide, her gaze is drawn to the house. The water, now lapping at her feet, appears to freeze her in that moment. A familiar, yet impossible ghosted figure stands on the porch. As if Eva, long since gone, is beckoning Willa to step inside.

The screened porch is on stilts, but the house sits on a stone foundation. Willa takes the path over the dune and through the sea grass to the stairs. A small handwritten sign hangs on the railing next to an overturned bucket: *Rinse Your Feet.* The steps to the porch, already hot from the morning sun, make her feet tingle with each step. Willa pushes the door open to see a rolled rug and a stack of folding chairs, along with baskets heaped with seashells. Wind chimes hang from the light blue ceiling. The porch's screen door into the main house is stuck on a high spot on the floor. Willa inserts the key to open the door to the house when the screen door lets loose and slams shut behind her, startling her.

Entering the cottage is like going back in time. It smells a little musty from being closed up. Eva's left all of the furnishings. There is a combined living room and kitchen, one bedroom and bath on the main level, and one bedroom and bath upstairs. The bathtubs are made of cast iron, with a curtain surrounding them for those who prefer to shower. The appliances are from the 1950s and complement the celery green cabinets perfectly, creating a retro vibe. There are no closets, but each bedroom features an armoire and floor-to-ceiling bookshelves containing an impressive library. Willa notices the grandmother's clock stopped at 4:10 and knows she must manually reset the clock's chains. Unsure of how to make it function, she decides to leave it in its idle state. She will have to learn how to set it to keep track of the minutes and the hours of her new life in this seaside home.

14

WILLA

As summer approaches, finding a job to cover her daily expenses is relatively easy for Willa. After arriving in New England, she interviews at an upscale restaurant and begins work immediately. Paul, her boss, assures her the tips will offset the low wages he offers.

Paul's mother, Claudia, teaches Willa a great deal about operating the kitchen equipment and the daily prep work required of the waitstaff. She likes to know she can depend on the staff for other functions in case someone calls in sick or doesn't show up for work.

A competent and quick study, Willa also learns that Claudia has doubts about Paul's ability to take over the business; as Claudia often mutters, "good for nothing," under her breath nearly every time Paul leaves the kitchen.

After just a few short weeks, Willa is tasked with closing the restaurant. Paul shows up and offers to help. She notices he has a fresh haircut and reeks of cheap cologne. He is peculiar, to say the least. Willa finishes closing the register and hands him the money pouch. Paul stands close to her, leaning on the counter, waving the money pouch, and says, "You could work anywhere you want with a body like that. In fact, you could become a prostitute and retire in ten years instead of waiting tables."

Willa can't believe he is so brazen. She has no intention of ever selling herself and thinks Claudia would be appalled to learn that her son has suggested such a thing.

Speechless, Willa hurries to leave. She can't unlock the front door fast enough to escape Paul and his bad advice.

Two days later, Willa begins work at another restaurant where the tips are twice as much, and she isn't required to do the prep work. Unfortunately, her new boss, Gilly, must have attended the same school of thought as Paul, because he regularly undresses her with his eyes. Willa finds herself having to decline Gilly's numerous requests to go for a ride in his Corvette. She tolerates him because the money's really good. After three months, Willa asks Gilly if she can have the weekend off to spend with a friend whom she's met at college. Gilly obliges her request.

Looking forward to the weekend, Willa is eager for Rich to see her place and show her around the area before he moves away. He has just completed community college and is preparing to start work at a graphic design agency in Connecticut.

Rich arrives at Willa's just before 11:00 a.m., and she motions for him to come inside. "This place is incredible!" Rich says, while his head swivels back and forth, taking in every inch of her cottage. "Oh WOW, and look at the view," he says, nodding with approval.

"Thank you. It is pretty great, isn't it?" Willa remarks, appreciating his enthusiasm.

"And look at these beautiful paintings." He studied each one stacked along the porch. "You never mentioned you are a painter."

"I like to dabble," Willa replies. Her stomach growls loudly from hunger. "I'm ready to go if you are? I skipped breakfast, knowing we're going out for lunch."

"I heard." Rich laughs. "Let's go."

They drive up the coast to a little lobster shack, where they enjoy lunch at a picnic table under a blue-and-white striped umbrella. Willa follows Rich's approach to shell and eat her lobster. Dipping each bite into drawn butter before savoring its sweet, delicate morsels.

"Thank you for introducing me to lobster," Willa says, licking the butter from her fingers. "I wasn't sure if I would like it, but I do. Have you ever tried mountain oysters?"

"I haven't. What are they? Do they taste like oysters from around here?" Rich asks.

Willa chuckles,"I wouldn't know. I don't eat oysters. At least I haven't up to this point in my life."

"I have so many questions. Like, what do their shells look like? What's the best season for them, and where do they come from, lakes?" Wanting to learn all about them, Rich fires questions.

Maybe she should've thought twice before asking Rich if he's ever tried mountain oysters. But then again, they did just sit and dismember a lobster to eat. Willa explains matter-of-factly, "Mountain oysters are bull testicles. They're served year-round, but the Oyster Roasts are popular during the ranching seasons. During the spring and fall round-ups, the herd gets branded and vaccinated, and the bulls get castrated for herd control."

Both inquisitive and somewhat repulsed, Rich hesitantly asks, "What do they taste like?"

Willa shrugged empathetically, "I really don't know. I've never tried them. I can't wrap my head around the idea of eating them when other food is available." And they both started laughing. "People seem to really enjoy them. They serve 'em for appetizers just like they do with the oysters here. Would you eat them?"

"I guess if it were me, I would at least try them, out of curiosity," replies Rich with a nervous laugh. "Let's drive back south, and I'll show you some beach access points off the beaten path. They're good to go, especially during the summer. Not a lot of tourists know how to get to them."

"Sounds good. I'm gonna miss seeing you at the campus bookstore and hearing your laugh in the hallways between classes." Willa tells him as they drive away from the restaurant.

"Willa, you're gonna be fine. I'm so ready to move on. Don't get me wrong, I love it here, but after three years, I need more, and I bet you will too." Rich says, waiting at a four-way stop to turn onto the access road tucked away in a neighborhood.

Suddenly, they hear sirens as police cars surround them. An officer asks Rich to step out of the vehicle. He puts him in handcuffs, claiming he's committed several traffic violations, including nearly hitting a police car and running multiple stop signs. He hauls him off to the police station.

Meanwhile, Willa is taken in front of the car and frisked, not by one officer, but by three. Once finished groping and sliding their hands all over her body, one at a time, Willa's ordered to drive Rich's car to the police station. She is trembling with fear and rage, and with no idea what they could've possibly done to warrant this situation. She knows they're false allegations. After two long hours, they release Rich with a citation and send them on their way. Petrified, they ride in silence. Their weekend comes to an abrupt halt, with Rich dropping Willa off at her cottage and going back to his apartment. It is the day before Willa's birthday.

Aside from Rich, she hasn't made any close friends and doesn't know who to talk with about what happened. Willa certainly doesn't feel like she can call her mom, as she'd insist Willa return home. Feeling violated, Willa sits holding onto me and sobs uncontrollably until she falls asleep on the couch.

The next morning, the sun wakes Willa with its bright light streaming into the living room. Still clutching me, her body aches from tension, but when she holds me up to the light, my color calms her, and she tucks me back into her pocket. Willa wraps herself in a blanket, makes a cup of tea, and carries it outside. Early mornings on the porch are part of her routine. Seeing the waves and smelling the salt air comforts her as she replays yesterday's events and wonders whether the police made a mistake, mistaking them for real criminals. But if that were the case, they wouldn't have issued Rich a citation. There's no rational explanation for what happened.

Willa goes back inside to get a second cup of tea and sees the bright yellow envelope on the counter. The card arrived last week, but she chose to save and open it on her birthday. Enclosed with the card is fifty dollars and the message, " I'm so proud of you for taking a chance, moving to Maine, and furthering your education. Love you bunches, Mom."

I love you too, Mom.

After finishing her tea, Willa brushes her teeth and sees her reflection in the mirror. This makes her think about a piece of advice she once read from a diplomat who makes it his daily practice to greet himself in the mirror every morning. He believes we should start our day by extending that courtesy to ourselves, just as we do to anyone we meet. And so Willa looks in the mirror and gives that new twenty-something a pep talk. The rest of the day, she combs the beach for treasures and tries to make sense of yesterday's debacle. It's good for her to occasionally engage with other beachgoers to make small talk or pet their dogs. The interaction helps Willa to escape her headspace. These walks are helpful when she is sometimes lonely or homesick after leaving Nebraska.

Willa returns to work on Monday morning to find Gilly with a Cheshire smile, opening the door for her and asking, "How was your weekend, honey?"

"It was horrible," Willa replies, rolling her eyes and not stopping to give him the time of day.

"What happened? I thought you were spending it with your boyfriend?" Gilly chided as he followed her back to the time-clock.

"Rich is not my boyfriend. He's a friend." Willa replies emphatically.

"So what happened? Why are you so upset? Did he hurt you?" Gilly asked, faking concern.

Willa relays the experience, and Gilly offers, "My uncle is a cop; let me see what I can do. Baby, don't worry."

Gilly approaches Willa before her shift ends and tells her he arranged for the local cop, his uncle, to void the citation, but the favor will cost her the exact amount of her paycheck. Naively, Willa agrees to this. The next day, the officer shows up in uniform in the back room at the receiving dock. Unaware of Willa's presence, she listens and watches him sell some joints he confiscated on a recent drug bust to one of the other employees. Gut-wrenched, she walks to the back entrance and hands him her signed paycheck without saying a word. In that moment, she realizes the whole thing has been a setup. The cop's eyes travel over and through her, and she wonders if he was one of the three who frisked her, but she will never know because they held her head to see nothing but the hood of the cruiser as they took turns feeling her up.

When Willa returns to the dining room, Gilly is there waiting.

"Wanna go for a ride in my Corvette? It'll make you feel better."

"No, Gilly, I don't. Not today. Not ever." Overwhelmed with disgust, she grips the sea glass in her apron pocket and walks out the door.

Willa calls Rich as soon as she gets home to share the news.

"Hi, Rich, it's Willa. I'll make this quick. My boss's uncle is a cop, and he was able to revoke your citation."

"Really? That's such a relief because I already have points from a speeding violation last year. I can't get any more points, or they'll suspend my license, and I won't be able to get to work. I've been so worried."

"I figured as much." Willa stated thoughtfully.

"Wow. Thanks so much. You know, something was really off about that whole thing."

"It was really creepy," she agreed. " I have to run, but I wanted to give you the news."

"Okay, and thanks. Hey, once I get settled in Connecticut, I'll be in touch."

"Okay, b'bye." Willa ends the call. Relieved Rich can't ask her any more questions.

15

SOPHIE

Beginning to establish her independence, Sophie finds a small, pet-friendly, rent-to-own cottage. It is only a short drive from the Colony where she works. Although it needs some serious TLC, the fenced-in yard will be great for Pence. Sophie spends the first week thoroughly cleaning the place. The windows are original with waves and imperfections in the glass, and the glazing is in dire need of repair. Something she would later do if she decides to purchase the home.

While vacuuming, she discovers that the house has very few electrical outlets, and the only overhead lighting is in the kitchen and bathroom. The uneven floors are worn from years of hard use and bear traces of where furnishings once sat. Sophie is reminded of the first home she and Eric purchased. Wanting a fresh start, they hired a crew to refinish the floors and give the interior a fresh coat of paint before they moved in. The thought of doing this now is tempting, but she isn't ready to make that kind of investment. Instead, Sophie decides the area rugs she brought with her will do for now.

The cat has taken up residency in an empty box under the kitchen table while Pence follows her from room to room as she unpacks boxes. Sophie sees he's struggling to get up and down and stops what she's doing to call the local vet, hoping he will prescribe something to help Pence. The earliest available appointment is three weeks out, but the receptionist has offered to add Sophie's name to the call list in case of an earlier cancellation.

Quickly acclimating to the area, Sophie likes that her new position affords her some anonymity as she adjusts to living alone for the first time since college. She's required to work occasional weekends and to take some online classes, which helps to offset the void she sometimes feels when loneliness creeps into her days.

Sophie's boss, Clayton Sutherland, also oversees the Colony's events. He ensures that Sophie is included in the upcoming Gala, allowing her to get a feel for the crowd responsible for sustaining this fiscally-sound artist retreat.

"Thank you for the invitation, Clayton," Sophie says as he walks into her office.

"This will be an excellent opportunity for you to meet our founders and benefactors. When you arrive, please come see me so I can make the introductions."

"I look forward to it. Thanks again."

"How are things going so far? Any questions?"

Sophie chuckles, "How much time do you have?"

"From what I've heard, you've hit the bricks running and are doing a great job." Clayton nods approvingly.

"I think things are going pretty well, but that's just my opinion."

Clayton smiles, "All's good. I'm off to my next meeting."

When Clayton leaves, Sophie immediately pulls the PR files from the previous fundraisers to learn more about this event. There are press photos with articles about special guests and featured speakers, prompting her to find out who will be in the spotlight this year. In preparation, Sophie reviews the guest list and makes some notes to help her with the introductions.

Later that afternoon, on her way out of the office, the sound of her cowboy boots on the wooden floor adds to her confidence. Her wavering thoughts of whether or not they're appropriate to wear to the Gala are diminished. After all, it is an artists' colony.

Every evening, Sophie takes Pence for a slow walk around the neighborhood. Within a couple of short weeks, Pence has started to stumble up the steps, and his breathing is much heavier. She is counting down the days until his veterinarian appointment. Only six more to go. Sophie rubs Pence's belly to reassure him before turning in for the night.

Awakened by the bright sunlight, Sophie pads her way to the kitchen to make coffee, stepping in a pile of poop. During the night, Pence must have lost control of his bladder and bowels in the house. She finds him lying next to the fireplace looking bewildered; he is unable to respond to Sophie's coaxing him to get up. She cleans up the reeking mess and calls the vet. They agree to see Pence right away. Fortunately, Clayton is completely understanding when she calls to explain and to let him know she won't be able to come to work.

The exam room door opens. "Hello, I'm Dr. Rubin. You must be Sophie, and this must be Pence. I've read his intake file and understand he's been having some mobility issues." Dr. Rubin gives Pence a few friendly strokes and begins examining him. Listening through a stethoscope, he tells Sophie, "Pence is in a very labored state of breathing. Unfortunately, at sixteen, his body is wearing down. Sophie, I can give you a couple of options. I can prescribe some meds that will keep him calm and somewhat comfortable. You can take him home and let this play out. I know this is a hard choice and not something you want to hear, but your other option is to have us administer a lethal injection so that he goes quickly and comfortably. Please, there's no rush to make a decision. Take some time to think about it, and I'll check back in with you."

Holding Pence's head in her lap on the examining room floor, Sophie weeps. How can she decide to end his life? Is this truly humane? She thinks of earlier this morning and the disgust she felt stepping into his feces and discovering the floors were soiled everywhere she looked. This is not the Pence she's loved for sixteen years. When Dr. Rubin returns, he crouches down to be with them.

"Have you made a decision?" he asks with compassion.

With tear-filled eyes, Sophie nods. I can't take him home like this. He's been such a good companion. I don't have the heart to watch him suffer."

Nodding in agreement, he responds, "I know it's really tough to lose a pet. For what it's worth, you're making the right decision. I'll have my team get prepared."

When they return, the yelping dogs from the adjacent rooms suddenly quiet as if they know what's about to happen. Sophie strokes Pence as he surrenders his last breath. Through his stethoscope, Dr. Rubin listens and confirms Pence is gone. Sadness envelops Sophie as she says her final goodbye.

"Sophie, I see in the file that you chose to have him cremated. Our office will call you when Pence's ashes are ready for pick-up," says Dr. Rubin as he walks her to the door.

Sophie's new position keeps her mind occupied during the day, but when she returns home from work, an emptiness remains. Pence no longer waits at the door to greet her, and even the cat sulks around in mourning. Pence's ashes are now in a beautiful wooden box on the mantle.

To fill her evenings, she begins to write poetry and prose. Reflecting on her life with Eric and the kids, writing becomes a rewarding and cathartic exercise when she lets her thoughts and insecurities fly onto the page. Sometimes laughing and sometimes crying her eyes out, Sophie begins to heal. The practice of becoming a wordsmith is so profound that it gives her the courage to write a letter to her children.

Dear Isla and Will,

As much as I relish our phone chats, I thought it was time to send you a letter. It's terrific that you are sharing an apartment while you adapt to living abroad. Having each other to lean on for company and support is good.

Speaking of support, I know you love Pence and the joy he's brought to our family. It is with great sadness that I'm writing to let you know he has gone to heaven. He's been such a great companion for our family and for me since the divorce. After sixteen years, I still expect to see him waiting at the door when I come home.

I recently accepted a position at the artist colony, which keeps me busy, and that really helps when I'm missing Pence. I'm happy to say the work makes me feel confident and present on all levels. Surrounding myself with inspiration and creativity has elevated my spirit. It's as if a light switch has been thrown "On." My desire to taste, breathe, and touch the world before me fills my soul.

As your mother, I sincerely wish to offer you a new and improved version of myself. Never for a moment do I regret the choices I've made, as each one has shaped the person I've become. Forgive me for not being fully present for you during those in-between years. I hope you will never have to go to the depths I did to find such happiness in life. I discovered I had a lot of healing to do. I've read many books and listened to theories about self-help and enlightenment, only to find that each method is as individual as we are; no two are alike. Similar, yes, but never the same. The process can become overwhelming if you let it.

For years, I've tried to find meaning and understanding in why things happen and how life events have shaped my response. Bottom line, it doesn't really matter! I'm being sincere. We can choose to hold onto ideas and rationalize our way into tomorrow. By doing so, it robs us of truly being in the moment. I hope you try to understand this early in life. I urge you to allow those you befriend and love to always feel safe and valued. To readily forgive those you love and yourself for the woulda, couldas.

Living without regret means you live every day with forgiveness in your heart. When frustration strikes, step away and imagine yourself wrapped in pure love and light. Say, "I forgive myself, and I forgive you". Look at yourself in the mirror and say it. Say it over and over again until it becomes a familiar habit. This was a hard lesson for me to embrace. I grew up misunderstanding forgiveness. I thought God was the only one truly capable of forgiving.

Last evening, I saw PhD Stephanie Mohonsky on PBS. Her lecture was on mindfulness and how we often blame others when we're unhappy. She realized that many of us need to acknowledge our subconscious feelings and bring them to the surface. I felt as though she was speaking directly to me. Ironically, when your father and I were together, I encouraged him to take her stress-reduction course. He reduced his high blood pressure by becoming more mindful of what's essential in life. This leads me to think about the qualities that attracted me to him: He's a strong, passionate, confident, creative, intelligent, and caring father; he loves the outdoors and enjoys good food and music. You must know you've inherited these qualities, and I marvel at your accomplishments daily.

There is no other reason than our shortcomings that caused him to walk away from our marriage. We weathered many storms and dug deep, trying to understand what happened to the love. Where did it go? My imperfections, including self-doubt and insecurity, were our biggest enemies. Those tendencies were like a disease. How long was Eric expected to care for me when what needed to be healed and nurtured had to come from within me? Your father was tormented by the non-validation of his continued attempts to make me happy. My insecurity led to a lack of trust, and our relationship spiraled down from there. Relationships are like gardens. It takes nurturing to bloom and grow, but you have to establish a good foundation.

I've forgiven myself and hope that you will understand and find forgiveness for me in your heart.

With My Eternal Love, Mom

How can I possibly reflect what the heavens provide through the sun, the moon, and the stars? Their light penetrates this opaque body of mine, while old souls search for wonderment through my eyes. I think of all the lessons I've learned, of love, and life, and loss. Acutely aware of their absence — I try with intention, with gratitude, to be the light.

16

SEA GLASS

There is an element of fight and resilience within all of us.
—Sea Glass

Despite her internal battle with low self-esteem, Sophie showed remarkable strength as a wife and mother. There were glimpses of her beginning to overcome her limiting beliefs. Her awareness heightened when she listened and learned from more confident people. Sophie began to consider the scope of forgiveness for others and for herself. I remember this because I was there. I was her pocketed touchstone, absorbing and releasing her tension, trauma, and self-doubt.

It's evident to me that Eric's sarcastic comments and desire to debate any topic often triggered a setback in Sophie's progress. Eric's well-read and can readily defend any subject, but Sophie's not wired that way. Her body recoiled in defense every time he challenged her in a discussion. While these spirited exchanges delighted Eric, she had no desire to be proven wrong again and again. Eventually, her thirst for conversations versus debates slowly led to withdrawal and Eric spending more time away from home. Making divorce a rational decision, but I'll never understand why she let me go, too. She couldn't have known how much it hurt when she abandoned me.

I understand the feeling of loss. At first, none of it made sense, and I felt numb. As those emotions began to thaw, I became angry. Furious. And after some time, my anger softened to sadness. As the days passed, I realized I needed to let go of grief, too.

Since Sophie's moved on, I've come to realize just how important it is to be nurtured and to shed negative energy. If we're lucky, we learn from our experiences, and I have.

The day Willa discovered me, I pulled myself up from the bootstraps. Her inquisitive desire to explore and learn gave me a new purpose. I was with her when she endured bullying and ridicule from her classmates. The girl's got some grit. Not to mention moving halfway across the country at the age of nineteen and being sexually harassed shortly after arriving in Maine. I may be her touchstone, but Willa was born with perseverance.

Community college is a good financial choice for Willa. Her savings are enough to buy her some time before she has to look for another job. Plus, it is an opportunity to leave the pettiness of high school behind and start anew. Although the courses are challenging, Willa finds them engaging: students want to be there, and the topics of discussion are stimulating and legitimate.

Professor Malicoat teaches the Literature and Writing courses, and his first assignment to the class is to write a short story about something they know. This exercise provides him with an overview of the students' writing ability. As Willa reflects on a topic to write about, she realizes she knows a lot about tools because her father taught her to use them in his woodworking shop. Willa writes about building a live-edge oak coffee table with him and how, metaphorically, he and the table shared characteristics. The professor is so pleased with her writing that he uses it as an example for the next class.

Inspired by the assignment, Willa applies for a part-time position at the local hardware store. Appreciating her knowledge of tools, Avery, the store owner, hires her on the spot. Willa is relieved to work for a woman after her wretched stint with the restaurateurs. As luck would have it, she has developed a customer following who often show up to purchase tools and accessories from Willa. These interactions at work and college help rebuild her confidence, putting the restaurant days behind her.

17

WILLA

Willa is thriving at the community college. Professor Malicoat encourages her to submit an application for the McGrady Colony Student Workshop. This cooperative agreement awards a scholarship to a student from the community to attend an intensive workshop to further their education. Unfamiliar with the Colony, Willa goes home and begins reading well into the night about the renowned reputation, history, and diverse talent of those who have attended the Colony to master their craft. Though flattered, she's intimidated and weary from the overload of information she's read. Willa turns the lights off and crawls into bed. While waiting to fall asleep, something within her suggests that if she applies herself, she too can become an emerging artist.

The following morning, Willa silences the quirky wind-up alarm clock on her nightstand. She purposefully chooses to limit her use of electronics not only in her bedroom but throughout the cottage. She does not own a microwave and rarely watches the small TV behind the cabinet doors. There are potted plants in every room to help purify the air while her phone is left to charge in the kitchen overnight. Willa goes directly to the shower, where she believes she does her best thinking. She compares attending the Colony to working at a hardware store, where she will learn about tools of the trade. Beyond her knowledge of woodworking tools, chats with builders, painters, and electricians provide her with a wealth of information she finds invaluable as a new homeowner. The idea of being immersed in the Colony and conversing with fellow writers convinces Willa to apply for the scholarship.

That evening, after returning from work, Willa completes the application. Taking a deep breath, she walks to the window to where her favorite view overlooks the ocean. Wrapped in her Aunt Eva's sweater, clutching a writing journal to her chest, she watches the waves. The moonlit tide is in, pounding the shore, and Willa's heart echoes. Never before has she dreamed like this.

18

SOPHIE

Liddy, it's good to hear from you; dinner sounds like a great idea. I'll drive over after work so we can catch up. Let's plan to meet at AJ's; they make a great whiskey sour," said Sophie.

Known for its homestyle comfort food, Sophie and Liddy arrive at the restaurant at the same time, looking forward to a relaxing evening and good conversation.

"Let's grab a drink at the bar while we wait for a booth to open up," suggests Liddy as she leads the way.

The restaurant has a fifties decor, with high-back, red leather booths, dark wooden tables, and Tiffany-style stained-glass lamps hanging above each one. The other tables are topped with matching red vinyl tablecloths and a glass overlay. Several tables are pushed together for a birthday party that is already well underway.

They take the last two seats available at the bar." You look good. It must be the new job is agreeing with you," Liddy says, holding her drink up with a nod to Sophie.

"I have to admit, it's going much better than I expected. I've been out of the workforce for some time, and I worried I couldn't adapt. It feels really nice to be back in New England. My co-workers at the Colony have been super helpful, including me in meetings so I can become familiar with the day-to-day operations and expectations," Sophie says in agreement. "Now, tell me about your pottery classes."

"I have some exciting news to share with you: I am finally opening my studio," Liddy says beaming.

"That is the best news. I am so happy for you," Sophie says giving her a squeeze.

"Plus, I already have students registered for classes for the next four months, and I was able to repurpose the barn as a classroom. Some neighbors helped me set it up, and my friends came over to install the kiln. You staying with me inspired me to go for it! Your confidence is contagious." Liddy says, feeling good about reconnecting with Sophie to catch up.

With just enough drink left in their glasses, they toast each other once more.

"It looks like they're cleaning our booth. Excuse me, nature calls. I'll join you at the table. If the waiter comes to take a drink order, I'll have a club soda with lime," Sophie says, leaving the bar.

She goes to the restroom and is surprised to find it available, given how busy the restaurant is. While there, Sophie checks her phone for messages. She finds another missed call from Eric. He was persistent; she'll give him that. Every Friday morning, he calls her, and every Friday, she refuses to answer.

Leaving the restroom, she notes the old photographs in the hallway. This establishment has become an institution in the community and is now operated by a fourth generation. She's happy to be there with a good friend, supporting the business.

Sophie approaches the wall of booths and looks down to see two men sitting side by side, holding hands with several empty glasses in front of them. As one of them set his oversized menu down, her eyes scanned upward to see their faces. Shaken with disbelief and rage, she bolts to find Liddy. "Let's get out of here, *now*," pleads Sophie.

Liddy threw $20 on the table, and they fled out the door.

"Sophie, what's wrong? What happened? Are the kids okay?" Liddy asks with great concern.

Heaving into the bushes next to the parking lot, Sophie's trying to catch her breath.

"Leave your car and let me drive you. I don't know how to help," Liddy tells her.

"Just… give …me… a moment," that is all Sophie could get out; her chest is pounding, and her head's racing.

They get into Liddy's car when Sophie asks, "Can we go to your place?"

"Of course. But shouldn't I take you to the doctor? This came on awfully fast."

"I'm not sick like that. Please, I'm begging you to get us away from here," Sophie bent forward, putting her head between her knees.

Liddy rolls the windows down for air, hoping to help calm Sophie. By the time they get to the house, Sophie has stopped crying and heaving, but is an emotional wreck. They sit in silence in a pair of old rockers on the porch, rocking. As time passes, the night air grows cooler, and Sophie becomes a little calmer. Liddy excused herself to go inside, returning with some blankets and a pot of tea.

"Thank you for being such a good friend," says Sophie.

"We've been through a lot, and whatever this is, we'll get through it too."

"Liddy, do you remember our chats years ago? When I felt something was off with Eric. The times when his best friend Conrad would always come to visit when I was away?"

"Yes, but I didn't think that was still a concern since you haven't talked about it in a long time."

"All of these years, I thought I was insecure or crazy. Even when I confronted Eric about specific people, he always denied it." Sophie spoke softly with a tone of disbelief in her voice, "I could tell he had fallen in love when he took his dream trip to Alaska. I could hear it in his voice. Naively, I thought he truly fell in love with the land. I loved him so much that I offered to let him go. Years later, I learned of the assistant fishing guide, a woman who had a reputation for obliging some of the fishermen in the camp when they thought they were safe to misbehave in the wilderness. E may have lost his fishing rod in the high grass. The two of them searched but never found it.

"Do you know how many times I've packed and unpacked his library when we relocate? It wasn't until this last move that I opened the beautiful, handmade book given to him when we lived here with the kids. I have handled that book with each move, but it caught my eye this time. There's a page marked with a feather, so I read it; a love letter from the person I'd suspected was his lover. The funny thing about that story is that I asked the Universe to send me a sign—a feather—if I was moving in the right direction. I never imagined a feather would lead me to the answer to a question I had so long ago." Emptying her glass, Sophie stops speaking and shakes her head. "There were so many times my gut would react, and I didn't listen to it. I kept pushing those feelings down, burying them. What does that do to a person over time? It must be damaging, like taking sips of poison," Sophie says, reflecting on those times.

"I'm so sorry you've had to deal with all of that. It sucks," said Liddy.

"It really does. You'll never believe who was sitting in the back booth at AJ's tonight."

"Who?"

"Eric," said Sophie, with disdain in her voice.

"What? I thought he was in Florida?"

Wiping tears from her eyes, Sophie tells Liddy, "As sure as I'm sitting here, I finally have proof. Eric and Conrad were beside each other, holding hands with their backs to the rest of the restaurant."

"Oh my God, no wonder you're a mess. Did you say anything to Eric? Hold on, before you respond, I think we'd better switch to wine."

"Great idea!" Sophie said, feeling the need to numb herself from deceit.

Liddy returns in a flash with the wine to hear the rest of the story. She barely takes a sip from her goblet to witness Sophie downing a glass of wine in one drink. Knowing her friend was hurting, she refilled Sophie's glass.

"What could I possibly say to him? 'You knowingly deceived me. You should've told me you're bisexual. I didn't deserve years of infidelity. I want a million-dollar life insurance policy, you bastard.' Taking another gulp, 'How could I possibly know who he's slept with or what he's exposed me to?' Sophie spewed.

Liddy thought it was best to remain silent and let Sophie get it off her chest, glass by glass.

19

SOPHIE

Disoriented, Sophie slowly sits up in bed. Was last night just a dream, a nightmare? Still in her clothes from yesterday, she makes her way downstairs to find Liddy coming in from the porch with two empty wine bottles in one hand and two goblets in the other. The reality of the situation feels immense to Sophie.

"Oh God... it really did happen." Sophie follows Liddy into the kitchen. "My gut was right, and I didn't listen to it. Was my entire marriage a lie? Did he use me as a cover-up? He used to come home from travels and be in a surly mood, not wanting to go out with me—all of those times when I felt diminished by his sarcasm. I remember him being nervous about me interacting with his colleagues, fearing I might use the wrong word or say something that would reflect poorly on him. I put such stock in that man that I believed it was true, that I wasn't sophisticated or intellectual enough."

Sophie's feeling so devastated that her body starts to convulse. She runs to the bathroom adjacent to the kitchen, vomiting into the commode. Facing herself in the mirror, she splashes water onto her tear-soaked, puffy face. The contrast between yesterday morning and now is unbelievable. Her tangled hair and bloodshot eyes appear as she pulls the towel down; holding it to her chest, she closes her eyes to steady her breath. She regrets drinking too much wine to numb her pain and anger.

Liddy points across the table to a tall glass of water with a couple of aspirin and some toast when Sophie comes back into the kitchen.

"Thank you." Sophie whispers weakly.

"It might help. I don't have any magic words or advice, but I will always be here for you. I checked on you a couple of times last night. I was a little worried when you stopped talking and nearly finished the second bottle. I'm here, and I'm not going anywhere." Liddy offered.

"Do you mean to say I didn't drone on and on all evening?"

"Friends don't need to say anything to be there for one another."

Thinking of last night, Sophie says, "I honestly don't remember how I made it up the stairs. I must have passed out once I hit the bed. And this was supposed to be a fun weekend for us."

"Once all of this is behind us, we can make plans for a fun weekend," Liddy said, patting Sophie's hand.

Sophie placed her other hand on top of Liddy's, "I'll hold you to it."

"Sophie, you deserve to be happy. When I was going through my divorce, I met with a counselor by the name of Alisha Pardon once every couple of weeks. She came highly recommended and helped me sort through my emotions. If you'd like, I can give you her number. Alisha's easy to talk to. She may even be able to give you some advice on how to break the news to Isla and Will. She really helped me and gave me some good advice."

20

SOPHIE

Good morning, Sophie. How can I help you?"

"Good morning, Ms. Pardon. Thank you for returning my call."

"I'm happy Liddy recommended me. Ninety percent of my clients come from referrals. Now, tell me a little bit about you?" asks Alisha.

Sophie begins by saying, "It's tough for me to share this with you, but I'll try."

"Go ahead, Sophie, I am listening."

"I discovered my husband, I should say, my ex-husband, is bisexual. I don't know how to live knowing that my entire marriage was a lie. I feel so violated, so angry, I want to spit," she says and breaks into an audible sob.

Alisha Pardon waits for a moment before asking, "Sophie, how did you find out about your ex?"

Taking a deep breath, Sophie tells Alisha, "I saw him holding hands with another man."

"Was that the first time you were confronted with his bisexuality?" Alisha asks.

Sophie begins, "Yes. Eric and I were married for twenty-five years, and once the children graduated from college, we decided to end it. As painful as it was, I felt responsible for our separation. I truly believed it's all because of my inadequacies."

Alisha asks to confirm, "You're telling me that you never suspected Eric to be attracted to other men?"

In an attempt to explain, Sophie says, "When we were kids living states apart, he and I both had a close friend who came out when they became adults. We both dated members of the opposite sex in high school, and when we met in college, there was definitely chemistry between us. Once we were married, my intuition would kick in. I could sense when he was attracted to other women. As a young couple, we had growing pains. Both of us had to work through issues of jealousy and insecurity. We had a pretty good partnership for about 15 years, but during that time, I was so busy working and raising our children that I didn't pay close attention to what was happening in our relationship.

"When Eric called me from Alaska, a trip he'd wanted to take since before we met, I could hear a change, a thrill, or pure joy in his voice as he finally arrived in Alaska. Then, the strangest thing occurred. Something within me shifted; I told him that I loved him so much and was grateful he was such a good father that I was willing to let him go and live the life he had always dreamed of having in Alaska. I couldn't imagine holding someone back from living their dream, not even my husband. I hung up the phone and felt entirely at ease, knowing I loved him enough to let him go. Forever changed, Eric did return home.

"I couldn't put my finger on it, but something felt off. I rationalized my feelings because of Eric's newfound love, Alaska. Years later, I learned of a woman who had been fired from her duties with the same guide service Eric used while in Alaska. Another fisherman, quite smitten with her beautiful blue eyes, told me she even wore a string of pearls along with her waders, and obliged the fisherman in the wilderness. I thought back to the photographs from his trip. She and Eric shared a raft. My intuition spoke when we stopped at a fly shop in Idaho several years later, and I witnessed the meeting of their eyes.

"You asked if I ever suspected his attraction to other men. Not really. The only time I ever confronted him with the possibility, he vehemently denied it. A woman knows intuitively when her husband has eyes for someone else. I struggled with how to react to my emotions. I would rationalize that he's human and can look as long as he didn't act on those feelings. But when it came to other men, I just thought he was infatuated by their success. Admiring them for their professional accomplishment."

Alisha asks, "Did something happen to cause you to confront him?"

"For a while, there seemed to be a pattern of Conrad, his one lifelong friend, showing up every time I left to visit friends or attend an event. I felt uneasy and finally gathered the nerve to approach the subject with Eric."

"How did he respond?"

"He was angry and completely offended that I would accuse him of being gay or bisexual. He turned the subject around and asked me if I was gay because I go shopping with my girlfriends," Sophie said as she pulled back and forth on her pendant necklace.

"Are you?"

"No. Eric was everything to me. I never looked at other men, let alone women, in the way that I saw my husband."

"Sophie, where did you leave the conversation?"

"I apologized to Eric, but he's not one to forget and rarely forgives. It's been over a decade, and he still joked about it in front of Conrad when he visited."

Alisha notes, "You're telling me he shared your private conversation with Conrad?"

"Apparently, he did. Talk about feeling awkward." Sophie takes a sip of water.

"Sophie, did you recognize the man Eric was holding hands with at the restaurant the other night?"

"Yeah, it was Conrad."

Alisha hears Sophie sobbing again. "This has been really tough, but do you recognize your intuition has been validated?"

"I do."

"What you've felt proved to be true. Now, it's my job to help you recover. Let's meet in person for the next session. For now, I would like you to keep a journal and record your feelings, emotions, and memories, both good and bad. Bring it with you next week, and we'll go from there. I'm going to offer some recommendations and provide you with some coping tools."

"But what do I tell my children? I've already written and told them I was the one to blame. That the divorce was all my fault, this is such a hellacious mess."

"You mentioned that when you called to make your first appointment. For now, we should focus on helping you; they're living life overseas. Allow yourself some time to process what you've been through. In time, you will be able to sit down with them and discuss this, but right now, it's much too raw. Your children will be better off learning this news once you're in a better place. I'll see you next Thursday at 10:15. Please bring your journal along. You have my number if you need to talk with me before then."

21

SOPHIE

Eric drove by the house while you were on the phone with Alisha," Liddy says. "I think he is looking for your car in the driveway. He's got some nerve. It's a good thing he didn't stop. I don't think I could've answered the door for him. If you're feeling up to it, we should probably go pick up your car this afternoon. You can put it in the garage while you're here."

"Liddy, if you don't mind, I just need to go back to my place and have time to myself before work on Monday. I need to collect my thoughts without worrying he might show up at your door looking for me. I can't bear the thought of him trying to fix this."

"I understand. I need to check on the kiln out in the shop. Come get me when you're ready to go get your car. There's some fruit and snacks on the counter and bottled water in the fridge if you want to take some for the drive back."

"Thanks. I'll go gather my things. I shouldn't be long."

22

SOPHIE

Relieved to return to her cottage, Sophie sets her overnight bag on the floor and is surprised when the cat comes over to circle her legs. She picks her up and cuddles her as she checks the auto-feeder to find that the cat food has been eaten, and there's still plenty of water in her bowl.

"You're starting to warm up to this place, aren't you?" Sophie says to the cat. Purring and content, the cat nudges Sophie's chin with affection.

The phone rings, and she juggles the cat to answer, "Hi, Liddy."

"Hi, I'm checking to see if your trip went okay?"

"Yes, I made it home safely. Thanks again for your support. Your friendship means the world to me."

"I know you'd be there for me if circumstances were reversed. I'm a phone call away if you need me."

"Thanks. I'll touch base with you to reschedule our Girls' Weekend.

"It's a deal. Love ya."

"Love you too."

The cat jumps from Sophie's arms and heads down the hallway to the bedroom. Sophie decides to go into the backyard to breathe in the last of the late afternoon. Hydrangeas and delphiniums are in bloom along the fence that surrounds the yard. Their shade of blue-green reminds her of the sea glass she once held dearly as her touchstone. In the far back corner is a mounded garden bed planted with hostas and orange day lilies surrounding a redbud tree. The plantings coax a feeling of nostalgia for Sophie as she reflects on the conversations and times she spent in the garden with Jacqui, a former neighbor. She taught Sophie the names of the perennials and which ones make good companion plants. When Sophie moved away from Dublin, she separated bulbs and plants, taking starts of them to establish a garden at her new home. The flowers represented the irreplaceable kinship that had grown between them. Jacqui was instrumental in helping Sophie discover that there's a woman within waiting to bloom. Although Jacqui has since passed, a wind chime hanging in the redbud tree begins tinkling on this still afternoon, and Sophie knows she's not alone.

23

WILLA

With the day off, Willa decides to take an early morning drive to the bakery. Just as she's about to open the door, it flings open, and there is Tilghman, looking as handsome as ever.

"Willa, it's good to see you!"

"Good to see you, too."

Stepping back inside, he asks, with what feels genuine to Willa, "How's it going? Do you like the area?"

Willa looks him in the eye and announces, "I am falling in love."

"Really, that was fast. With who?" Tilghman asked. Surprised by his initial reaction of feeling a tad disappointed that Willa had fallen in love with someone.

"I'm in love with the ocean."

"Oh?"

"I continue to be amazed by how it's constantly changing every day, every time of the day. My cheeks actually hurt for the first week I was here because I was smiling so much. I had no idea what I was missing in my life. I don't think that I could ever live anywhere else."

"Wow. You're not kidding. I'm glad you're so happy. I guess when you grow up here, it kind of loses some of its magic. I've grown accustomed to the tides and everyone knowing everybody's business. But I'll admit, there's nothing quite like sailing at sunset. That never gets old for me."

Willa appreciates the passion in his voice. "Do you sail often?" She asks.

"Every chance I get. Have you been?" Tilghman inquires.

"No. Not yet."

"I'll tell you what: If the weather holds, I'm planning to go this weekend. Would you like to come along?"

"I would love to, but I'm working till noon on Saturday."

"That's fine. I have to be at a closing on Saturday morning anyway. Why don't you plan to meet me at Joe's Marina, say 3:00?"

"I'll be there. Tilghman, what should I bring?" Willa asks.

"Just bring yourself and that sense of adventure. I have the necessities on the boat. I'm sorry, but I have to run. My Dad's in the office this morning and is a stickler for punctuality. See you Saturday."

"I look forward to it." Willa says, noticing his broad shoulders as he turns to leave.

In a state of disbelief at her good fortune, Willa feels like she is floating out of the bakery. She sits down at one of the café tables to soak up the sunshine and enjoy her pastry when the wind kicks up, sending the newspaper from the man sitting at a table across from her onto her feet. Willa secures her plate with one hand and reaches down to retrieve his paper for him when the headline catches her attention: "Local Businesses Investigated for Human Trafficking," instantly triggering visceral chills.

"Good morning. Thank you for catching my paper in the wind."

She looks up to hand the newspaper to the plain-clothed man now standing in front of her, noticing an official badge clipped to his belt.

24

SOPHIE

Everyone at the Colony is in full swing, preparing for the Gala. Clayton agrees to let Sophie work a half-day on Thursday in exchange for her working the extra hours needed on the days leading up to the event. She is relieved to be able to keep her appointment with her counselor.

Arriving at Ms. Pardon's office 30 minutes early gives her time to sit in her car and reread the notes in her journal. Her hands begin to tremble as her chest tightens. There's a lot of anger and rage in those few pages; she isn't proud of it or how it makes her feel. Throughout her youth, Sophie was conditioned to keep her emotions in check. She was expected to harness her emotions and behave like a young lady.

Sophie enters the office to find the waiting room decorated in very calming hues of sandstone and light turquoise. Large potted peace lilies sit on the floor before the open windows, allowing fresh air to flow into the room. She steps in front of a photograph to check her hair in the glass. As she adjusts the out-of-place strands, she's taken aback—it's a beach scene with shells and sea glass washed up against a piece of driftwood. Reminding her of their family trip to Ogunquit and her discovery of what became her talisman. Her good luck charm.

Alisha enters the room and welcomes Sophie. "I love to go beach combing, so my friend gifted me the photograph when I opened my office. I don't get to the beach very often anymore, but it's a nice reminder. Come on in."

Sophie has never been to a counselor's office before and doesn't know what to expect as she follows Alisha into her office.

"It's nice to meet you face to face, Sophie."

"Likewise."

If Sophie were to guess, Alisha is probably in her late forties. Her pixie hairstyle accents her stunning blue eyes and small stature. Dressed in business casual, Alisha's presence puts Sophie at ease. Alisha takes a seat across from

Sophie rather than sitting behind her desk.

"I see you brought your journal. Has recording your thoughts since our last appointment been helpful?"

"I am embarrassed to admit that it's filled with rage. Rereading it makes me angry all over again."

"Why do you feel embarrassed?"

"Honestly, I wasn't raised to hold such contempt in my heart. Whenever I got angry, I was taught that it wasn't very becoming and to let it go."

"But those feelings are real and shouldn't be suppressed. First, you need time to sit and acknowledge them. This gives you the opportunity to understand why you're feeling anger or resentment. Once you gain that understanding, it's easier to release those feelings so that you may heal."

"I think I should burn those pages."

"For now, I'd like you to keep them to mark your progress. How are you feeling emotionally right now?"

"I feel lost. Accepting that I was the cause of our marriage ending was hard, but I did. But when I discovered Eric betrayed me throughout our marriage, I lost trust in myself. I've lost my compass."

"Does this impact your ability to function day to day?"

"It does, but I try my best not to let it. I started working, and so far it's going well. It's a small staff, so we are swamped with work most days. I sometimes choose to work on the weekends, and that helps to fill the void and keeps my mind occupied so that I don't dwell on my failed marriage."

"Besides work, do you have any other tools or practices to help you cope?"

"I call a good friend, meditate, or do some Reiki energy work. I'm due for a good massage."

"All of those are beneficial. Tell me, how does this betrayal impact your day-to-day life when you're not working?"

"I feel like he took advantage of me. I find myself thinking about how most of the household tasks and raising the kids fell on me because Eric often traveled for work. While it has made me stronger and more independent, I do feel some resentment."

"Did you ever feel appreciated for your contribution to the marriage?"

"Sometimes." Sophie pauses for a moment before she continues. "I didn't know who I was supposed to be for Eric. I tried to keep up my appearance and take care of our home for Eric, but it became, *My Thing*."

"Your *Thing*?"

"Yes. I discovered we have different Love Languages. Well into our marriage, what we thought we were doing as an act of love for one another ended up not validating what either of us needed. Our marriage became a situation where neither of us felt valued by the other. Eric rarely complimented me or noticed the improvements or repairs I did at home. When I'd bring something to his attention, he'd shrug and say, "That's your thing." I rationalized his response to the fact that he was coming home from traveling or that his workload kept him preoccupied."

"You said neither of you felt valued by the other?"

"Right. Eric thrives on accolades and gifts, but that validation doesn't come naturally to me. I thanked him for working and providing for our family, but it wasn't enough for him. Do you think my childhood has anything to do with this?"

"Sophie, I will ask you to trust me as we move forward. I want to help guide you through this healing process, but we are not going to approach it as if you are a victim."

Shifting in her seat, Sophie wasn't sure how to respond.

"We will focus on you, your awareness, and how to begin living your truth."

Noticing Sophie's discomfort, Alisha says, "It's a nice day. Why don't we take a walk and continue our conversation?"

The sidewalks are dappled with sunlight, and the air is scented with freshly mowed grass as the landscape crew finishes mowing in front of the Library next door.

"It's comforting for me to come back here."

"I didn't realize you lived here before, but that makes sense since you're friends with Liddy. You mentioned that you meditate. Is meditation your form of prayer?"

"Yes. I've always believed in God or a higher power."

"Do you pray to God?"

"I do."

"Do you have any religious affiliation?"

"I haven't attended church in years. When I was a kid, we attended a Methodist Church with our mother. My father was an altar boy for a Catholic church when he was young, but he rarely attended church with us. My aunt, uncle, and cousins were Jehovah's Witnesses. I think that's when I first became aware of the struggle between organized religions. In my heart, I never believed God would make us choose one religion over another, and I don't believe we're here to suffer."

"I agree with you. Tell me, what do you know about Reiki?"

"I'm no expert, but being introduced to Reiki was like a crash course in exploring our body's energetic fields. I learned about Auras and Chakras, and where we hold pain in our bodies. Reiki introduced me to my ability to tap into a deeper level of prayer. It's as though I'm actually able to connect with God's higher power. Have you ever tried it?"

"I don't label it Reiki, but I do know the healing power of prayer."

"Have you ever experienced the feeling of a light source within?" Sophie asks. "It's incredible. I remember one session when I told the practitioner that I really liked the heat lamp she had placed above me while I was lying on the massage table. I felt as though I was basking in the sun. My whole body was illuminated and at peace. I opened my eyes at the end of the treatment to see her smiling at me. Nothing was there. There were no windows for sunlight to come in. She thanked me for being open to receiving light."

"Do you have a specific meditation routine or practice?"

"Not really. I do it randomly when the urge strikes. For instance, I prayed about finding a job and a place to live. I also pray for my kids' and friends' well-being, but I don't have a set schedule."

"Sophie, you're ahead of the game when it comes to healing. Your openness to discussing God and your experiences suggests you are willing to consider what some consider unconventional practices. I'd like you to take the next three weeks to establish a morning meditation habit. Start with five minutes a day and restart if you get distracted by random thoughts. Let's see if you can build up to 15 minutes, or more, inviting God into your heart with your soul focused on you. I want you to establish a ritual to cultivate awareness and focus. Afterward, record your thoughts and discoveries in your journal. Here's a little tip. Before you go to sleep, tell yourself you'll meditate every morning. It's a way to put those intentions into action."

As they walked back to Alisha's office, Sophie pondered her assignment. Alisha's reassurance gave her hope.

"Thank you for coming. I look forward to our next walk."

"Thank you. I'll give it a try and see what happens. I appreciate you juggling your schedule so I can come during lunch. With my new job, I don't have the flexibility to request time off in the mornings."

"I understand. I'm happy it works out."

Sophie noticed her journal no longer carried the weight it did when she arrived for her appointment.

25

SOPHIE

Good morning, Clayton," Sophie says, greeting him as he walks into her office, handing her a leftover bouquet.

"Good morning. They're too beautiful to throw out. I thought you might enjoy them a little longer." Clayton says as he pops down in a chair for a quick visit. "So, you survived your first McGrady Gala. Did you enjoy yourself?"

"I can't thank you enough for including me; it was a spectacular evening. I heard several guests remark that this year's event exceeded their expectations. You set the stage for a grand gala, and grand it was." Sophie replied, still beaming from the event.

"Jaimie's idea to use herbs from our own gardens mixed with wildflowers for the centerpieces saved us a lot of money, and they were exquisite. We came in under budget yet made it beautiful, and what donor doesn't appreciate fiscal savvy?" Clayton boasted.

"The guests really appreciated her sharing the backstory of the herbs, their meaning, and why they were purposely selected for the arrangements. I loved that she selected rosemary to signify remembrance for the community of artists and donors who founded the colony, and thyme, a symbol of strength, to attract love and riches." Sophie adds, "The Colonies' mission to value art and support the growth of artists speaks right to my heart. I feel so lucky to be here."

"It is a special place," Clayton adds in agreement.

"Did you know both McKenzie's and Bower's have working studios? Elizabeth McKenzie is a jeweler, and Jeremiah Bowers is a plein air artist. It makes me wonder how many of our donors are artists?" Sophie asks excitedly.

"I don't know the answer to that, but I do know that most of our donors made their fortune in other businesses. Their success has enabled them to become collectors and contributors, and to have their own backyard studios."

"Interesting." Sophie sat back amazed.

"And you could've heard a pin drop during Jo Jo's keynote. Her speech was as captivating as her music. Assigning the different guest tables to woodwinds, brass, percussion, and strings to demonstrate how everyone contributes to the song, or in this case, 'The Colony,' was a brilliant move. Her humble story was the perfect example of how the world rewards us with abundance when we give generously from the heart."

Checking his Cartier watch, Clayton tells Sophie, "I have to go. I can't be late for the post-gala benefactor meeting. Before I go, are you on target for the student workshop orientation? You'll have help, so it's mostly organization and scheduling on your part."

"Yes, I believe so." Sophie says as she holds up her crossed fingers.

"Great. I'll be available after the meeting if anything comes up." Clayton states, while tugging the cuffs of his sleeves to show evenly under his sport coat.

26

WILLA

It's a rainy Saturday morning, and Willa is opening the store. Her morning routine involves turning on the lights and music, preparing the cash register with cash from the safe, washing the glass on the front door, unlocking it for business, and setting the specials and promotions board on the sidewalk. She also waters the flowers in the whiskey barrels that flanked the entrance and puts the "Open for Business" flag in its holder. If time allows, she restocks shelves in the front near the store's register.

Willa recalls the bell that announces visitors at the Goodwill store and suggests they use one at the hardware store. Her boss, Avery, likes the idea and finds a pair of thick leather straps with brass bells in their Christmas decor inventory to hang on the front and back doors. Now the entry of both visitors and deliveries can be heard by anyone in the store.

The lingering drizzle keeps people home this morning, making time go by slowly. Willa is hoping the weather will clear by the time she's to meet Tilghman at the marina for her very first sailing experience. She went down to the marina the morning he invited her. Excited to explore and observe the happenings of a marina, she wanted to know where to go in advance of their date. *It's not a date. It's just an outing,* she reminds herself.

Daydreaming, the thought of Tilghman's invitation makes her giddy again. Bells sounding from both directions snap Willa's attention back to reality. Roz, the UPS driver, is coming up the center aisle with a delivery on a hand truck while Carol from Tilghman's office enters the front door.

"I had no idea you worked here," Carol said, scanning the aisle directories.

"Good morning, Carol. How can I help you?"

"I need some light bulbs for the office. Tilghman and his father prefer that all of the lights be soft white, not the blueish LED ones I put in their desk lamps. I thought I was doing them a favor by brightening their workspace."

"They're in aisle five. Would you like me to help you find them?"

"No, dear," she snipped, "I'm quite capable of finding a lightbulb."

Carol lays her phone face up on the counter as Willa begins to ring up the light bulbs. Willa sees the call notification with the name Gilly appear on the screen as Carol reaches for the phone. Carol answers the call and lays a $100 bill on the counter, grabs the bag of light bulbs, and quickly turns to leave without taking her change.

Willa follows her down the sidewalk to hear Carol say, "Gilly, I swear to you, if the FBI comes knocking on my door, I won't protect you again. You promised me you wouldn't get involved, and now it's making the front page." She feels a tap on her shoulder. *A news reporter?*

"Excuse me, Carol?"

"What do you want...more importantly, what did you hear?"

"You left in such a hurry, I brought your change and receipt."

Flushed with crimson, Carol holds out her hand, "I had to take an important call from the office. Thanks for running after me with the change."

"You're welcome." Willa turns, stunned to think Ms. Prim and Proper Carol could be connected to the man responsible for sexually harassing her.

27

WILLA

Glad to find the storm front has moved on. Tilghman arrives early in the afternoon at the marina. Like his father taught him, he follows a checklist to prepare the boat. Spending time on the water comes naturally to him. He checks the tide schedule and forecast to determine which direction to go. It is 3 p.m. on the dot when his phone rings. "

"Hi Willa. Where are you?"

"I'm here, but I don't know which dock to go to or where to find your boat." Willa responds eagerly.

"I'm over at B Dock, Slip 14, but I'll meet you at the store. I want to grab a bag of ice for our trip. I'll be right there."

The marina store is hopping with kids, captains, and tourists. Outside, the bicycles are stacked two and three deep in the rack, with kids in line for ice cream. The warm afternoon smells briny, but when she steps inside, the air is layered thick with the scent of suntan lotions. Willa grabs a bag of saltwater taffy and some water when Adonis, aka Tilghman, walks into the store. Taking her breath away with his tousled hair and unbuttoned shirt, revealing his sun-tanned body.

"Nancy," Tilghman calls out over the people waiting in line to one of the women at the checkout. "Can you add these," pointing to her water, taffy, and a 10-lb bag of ice, "to my account?"

"Sure thing, Baby." She smiles, motioning him on.

Smiling from their exchange, Tilghman holds the door for Willa.

"Wow, it must be nice to have clout?"

"Nancy's family and mine have been friends forever. It's easy for them to bill the account since I have a boat slip. You look great, by the way. You're dressed like you've sailed before — must come naturally."

"I'm not sure about that, but thank you," relieved to know she had made a good first impression. She'd have to thank her boss Avery for the wardrobe recommendation.

As they approach B-Dock, Willa notices the boat names and asks, “What’s the name of your boat?”

“Sun Dog.” He says with a grin. “Here we are,” Tilghman announces. Stepping onto the boat first, he turns to assist Willa aboard.

“Why Sun Dog?” She takes his hand and steps down onto the deck.

“The day before I took the bar exam, I did some soul-searching. I was feeling the pressure to pass the exam, so I took an early morning walk out onto the pier in the bitter cold of February and tried to envision myself as successful as my father. The weather conditions just happened to be right for this phenomenon to occur. While on the dock, I saw an amazing sun dog appear. The light refracting on the crystallization that morning was outstanding. Some people believe that if you see one, it brings good luck or good fortune. This sounds silly, but seeing it made me feel I would do fine. It felt like reassurance.”

“And...?” Willa coaxes him to tell her more.

“My father was so proud of me when I passed the bar exam that he went halves with me on the boat, and I knew I had to name it Sun Dog,” Tilghman replies, noting the hazel color of Willa’s eyes.

“I used to see sun dogs in Nebraska, but it was rare,” Willa said.

“You’re one of the few people I’ve met who’s heard of them.”

“That’s a really cool background story of how you selected a name for your boat. If I were going to name a boat, I think I’d call it Sea Glass.”

“Really? Why Sea Glass?” He asks.

“It’s my lucky charm, I found it in Nebraska.”

“Nebraska, of all places. I wasn’t expecting that. I hope you brought it with you since it’s your first time sailing,” he grins.

“Actually, it’s right here,” tapping her shorts pocket.

“I’d like to see it once we’re out on the water. Let’s secure your bag in the compartment under this seat. Here’s a life vest if you’d feel more comfortable wearing one. Otherwise, you’ll know where they are if needed. I’ll give you a quick tour and safety briefing, and then we’ll be on our way.”

“I’m really looking forward to this adventure,” she says, squeezing Sea Glass with one hand in her pocket and holding onto her life vest in a death grip with the other. She notices the people on the other boats opted not to wear life vests, giving her the jitters.

Tilghman’s proficiency in steering the boat away from the dock and into the open water eases some of the anxiety she is trying her best to hide. Within minutes, the voices at the marina fade, giving way to the lulling roll of the water and the summer breeze. Tilghman hoists the mainsail and mizzen sails, unfurls the jib, and cuts the engine. Taken by the quietness, Willa leans back in her seat. The sun and salt air are freeing. Doubts and fears, to-do lists, all vanish. It is an inexplicable moment of pure bliss as she watches the shoreline stretch before her.

"Would you like something to drink? I have water, soft drinks, beer, and wine."

"I'll have an iced tea if that's an option."

Tilghman pops open the can, "Here you go."

Willa watches him take a long draw of water from his cup, noticing the small tattoo on the inside of his wrist. It is a smaller version of the Sun Dog logo on his boat.

"We'll head up along the coastline for a little while to give you a view from the water. Does that sound good to you?"

"Yes, I'd like that."

"We're in for a great time on the water. Where's that lucky charm?" Tilghman asks with a bit of tease in his voice.

"Oh, it's just something I found as a little girl. I loved its color and discovered it was a piece of sea glass. I've carried it with me for years. When you live in Nebraska and you've never been to the ocean, sea glass seems exotic and full of possibilities. I have always wondered where it came from. I dreamed of visiting the ocean one day. Then, when my aunt left me her cottage, it became even more magical. You probably think I'm crazy, but it's almost as if it's led me here to Maine." Willa hands him the sea glass.

"You're right, it is a very pretty color. I'm not sure I've ever seen that color of glass before. There are lots of places along the coast where people collect sea glass and shells. Maybe one of the local shopkeepers could help you identify it."

"Good idea!" Willa said, surprised by his interest.

He hands the sea glass back when Willa lightly touches his wrist and remarks, "I noticed you are wearing your good luck charm."

At the helm, Tilghman nods. He looks at Willa, and their eyes meet. "Yeah, it keeps me grounded. I'm grateful," he says, dropping his sunglasses back onto his face and looking ahead. Willa wonders if he felt it, too. The electric charge that instantaneously caused butterflies in her stomach. She immediately puts on her sunglasses too, so as not to be a dead giveaway, and tightly holds onto the sea glass in her pocket to ride out this feeling.

As they pass by other boats, Tilghman appears popular, waving and chatting as he navigates the water. According to Tilghman, the boating community is well-connected and looks after one another on and off the water.

"You surprised me when you said you worked at the hardware store. Weren't you going to attend community college?" asks Tilghman.

"Well, I do both," Willa replies. Obviously, Tilghman didn't have to work while in law school. Lucky guy. "I'm putting myself through school, so even though I have a place to live, I need to cover my expenses, taxes, and tuition," Willa explains.

"That's admirable, but I doubt Avery can afford to pay you a decent salary," Tilghman says with a bit of attitude.

Ah, the town where everybody knows everybody's business. Willa stiffens up.

Noticing Willa's body language, Tilghman says, "I didn't mean to sound disparaging. I just know you can make a ton of money in a short amount of time, waitressing at one of the upscale restaurants in town. The tips are great. Some of my friends used to work three months in the summer and were financially set for the entire school year. It's only a suggestion."

Goodbye, butterflies, hello, nerves. I barely know Tilghman. I can't tell him what happened to me."Thanks. I did try a couple of waitressing jobs, but they weren't a good fit for me. Maybe it's because I'm not accustomed to the food or the folks that flock to these coastal areas in the summer," Willa says, casually passing it off, yet triggered by memories of her former bosses.

"That's a valid point. I'm sure once you're here for a while, other doors may open up. Let me know if I can put you in touch with anyone." Tilghman responds with kindness for the remainder of the sail. Willa purposely asks questions to keep the conversation about him, to which he seems comfortable sharing.

"You have a beautiful boat, or is it a yacht?" Willa asks.

"Thanks. Technically, anything over 40 feet is considered a yacht, and this is a 42-foot Whitby Ketch." Tilghman said.

"Why did you pick this one?" Willa asks, as she runs her hand over the smooth teak.

"It belonged to my grandfather, who died before I started school. The story goes that it was dry-docked for decades, and they forgot to include it in their trust, so when my grandmother passed away, I bought it at her estate sale. It needed a lot of work to bring it back. Almost two years' worth. When I reviewed the logbooks and paperwork, there was no indication that it had been given a name. We were restoring the teak galley and updating the wiring at Martins when Oliver, one of the guys at the shop, told me that my grandfather had been given the boat in exchange for legal fees. Oliver's got to be in his nineties; he couldn't remember who made the deal. That may be why it's been in storage all those years. Either that or because my grandmother's deathly afraid of the water." Tilghman said, shrugging his shoulders.

"And here you are, completely comfortable sailing your very own yacht." Willa remarks.

"There's something about the original craftsmanship and the attention to detail that I just love. Come here and hold the wheel." Tilghman says, taking his sunglasses off. He invites her to stand with him.

Willa stands to take hold of the large wheel, and Tilghman places his hands upon hers. With bright eyes, he asks, "Tell me, doesn't it feel like the whole boat comes alive?"

The closeness and warmth of his body, combined with the clean, natural scent of his cologne, render Willa momentarily speechless.

"Wow. It feels incredible." Trying to regain composure, Willa steps aside and asks, "Is everyone in your family a lawyer?"

"We have quite a few," he chuckles. "Our family get-togethers usually include a spirited debate or two." Tilghman responds, noticing Willa has become much more relaxed.

The temperature drops as the sun is nearly erased from the horizon. Tilghman eases the boat back into the slip and secures the lines. Grabbing a beer from the cooler, he says, "Thanks for coming out today. I hope you've had a good time." He reaches out from the dock to help Willa step off the boat.

"Tilghman, I had a very nice time. I'll admit I was a little nervous, but I was okay once I saw that life jacket and how easily you handle the boat. It also helped when I discovered everyone around here knows you! I didn't think you'd throw me overboard," Willa jokes.

"Next time, we can sail past your place so you can see it from the water." Tilghman said.

"That would be fun. Thanks again."

"I'll see you around. I need to stay and button up some things. It's such a beautiful night; I might sleep on the boat," Tilghman waves to her and steps back on board.

Next time, Willa thinks as she walks back to her car, seriously hoping Tilghman is not involved with GIlly.

28

WILLA

Willa rolls the windows down for the drive home from the marina. There are only four stoplights in town, but traffic is heavy on Saturday nights. While waiting for the light to change, the aroma from Palo's Pizza Shop on the corner fills the air, causing Willa to want a big slice of their Margherita pizza. She slips into Avery's parking spot, located behind the hardware store next to Palos. It is after hours, and Willa knows Avery wouldn't mind.

Willa announces as she's coming through the door with a bounce in her step, "You guys make the best pizza! Do you have any slices of Margherita?"

"Eli, how long will that Margherita take?" Tony shouts, giving Willa a wink.

"Two minutes, Tony. Two minutes." Eli yells, tossing a round of dough above his head.

"Great! I can pay now if you'd like." Willa offers.

"It's on the house tonight." Tony says while boxing to-go orders.

"It's my lucky day. What's the occasion?"

"Eli's wife called and said she's going to have a baby girl. Anyone who comes in tonight and orders a Margherita pizza gets a complimentary pie. It's how we do things here. We're family."

Willa smiles and says, "I always tell people at school and work that you make the best pizza."

"That's it, Honey. Our business thrives on word of mouth. Do you want some hot peppers or garlic added to your pizza?" "

"Not tonight. Thanks again."

"Good to see you," Tony says, handing her the box of pizza.

Willa puts a tip in the jar and takes the pizza home. She sits on the back steps of the cottage to enjoy it while watching the waves. Thinking about Tilghman and how different her life could have been had she grown up in his world.

She pulls the sea glass from her pocket, and as she touches it, she swears she can feel Tilghman's energy. As if his hand were atop hers like it was at the wheel of his yacht, stirring a feeling deep within. She closes her eyes, and a vision of the two of them appears. She is at a train station with their daughter waiting to greet him when he steps off the train dressed in a WWII army uniform. This vision leaves her with the distinct impression that they were soulmates from a previous lifetime. The ping of her phone interrupts her trance. It's a message from Tilghman. She reads—*You were great company today, but we talked more about me than you. Sorry. I'd like to learn more about you, so let's plan to get together soon. I spend a lot of my free time on the boat; you're welcome to stop by anytime.*

29

WILLA

"Welcome to the Colony! I'm Sophie, tell me your name and I'll get you checked in."

"Willa Jessop."

"Here you are," Sophie says, handing Willa a packet of information. "You had a bit of a drive to get here. Did you have any difficulty finding us?"

"My drive was fine. In fact, it was absolutely magical driving down the lane to the Colony. I love how the giant maple trees create a tunnel over the lane, opening up to the meadow with the sheep and the mountains in the distance. It was as if a story was unfolding before me. I can't believe I'm here," Willa answers.

Feeling Willa's excitement, Sophie says, "I know exactly what you mean. I felt the same enchantment when I drove down the lane for the first time, and I still do. The first session will start in about 30 minutes in the Evenger Meeting Room. Here's the key to your cabin. We ask guests to leave their cars in the main lot and walk to their cabins; it's part of the artistic immersion we encourage while staying here."

Willa parks and follows the path to her cabin, noticing that the sounds and scents are different from life on the coast and in Nebraska. She opens the rustic door to O'Keefe's Cabin to find a welcome basket of snacks and drinks waiting for her. The cabin has a small desk with a lamp, a full-size bed, and a bathroom. The wooden threshold is worn, and so are the floors. The curtains are fastened to the side of the open windows. She sets her belongings down, grabs her notebook, and heads back to the meeting room, eager for this experience.

After the Introduction, they separate into groups of writers, musicians, and mixed-media artists to meet with their team leaders/mentors. Mr. Newton leads their small class of four writers to the pavilion overlooking the herb and vegetable gardens. He shares that in addition to leading workshops, he oversees the gardens that provide sustenance for visiting residents of the colony.

"Class, I'd like you to step into the herb garden and note the fragrances. Take a pinch of a plant, rub it between your fingers, and put it to your nose. Close your eyes and smell it again. Taste it. What do you think of, hear, or see? Does the scent remind you of something, someone? You've been selected for this workshop because someone believes you have the potential to become a writer. A good writer. I want you to prove them right. I want you to take this opportunity to shine. Now that we've done a little sensory awakening, I'd like you to take this afternoon to write. I want you to dig deeper and give me something to consider. Tell me something you know. Tell me something about you. We'll reconvene at 5:30 in Bancroft Hall to listen to your writings before dinner. The hall is next to the dining room, which is directly across from where you registered today," Mr. Newton informs the class.

Mitchell, a lanky classmate with character-worthy features, speaks up, "Tell us about you."

Newton smiles, his eyes brighten. "I've spent my entire life writing. You can read all there is to know about me on my website. I encourage all of you to read—not just my website, but everything you can get your hands on. The more informed you are, the better writer you will be.

Audrey, with a head of flaming red untamed curls, standing next to Willa, asks, "What are you expecting, a story, a paragraph, a sentence?"

Newton kindly responds, "The choice is yours."

With about an hour to write, Willa opts to sit at a picnic table under the pines next to the main house. Suddenly, she's slapping a swarm of mosquitoes away from her body and can't focus on her writing. Panicked, she runs back to her cabin, searching for the cortisone in her bag to relieve the itchy swelling bites. Once Willa feels some relief, she writes a short paragraph for the assignment before meeting with their mentor.

Bancroft Hall, also known as the common area, is anything but common. It is a world unlike any Willa has ever known. She can hear them, the other artists, in conversations, while the sounds of dishes clanking come from the staff preparing the dining room. The grand piano, the images adorning the walls, and the books on the Colony's history and guests clearly indicate this refuge has cultivated greatness. Standing there, Willa allows her hands to rest on the pages of thoughts recorded; she dreams. Filled with emotion, something unexplainable is happening. Her heart is awakened, and there is no wind to carry this emotion; for this moment, she breathes it in.

And then she feels the presence of someone.

"Willa?"

"Hi, Sophie."

"You looked lost in thought."

"Actually, I was. I'm feeling a bit overwhelmed with the thought of being here." Willa says.

Feeling maternal, Sophie says, "Please, you have every right to be here. If I may make a suggestion, rather than comparing yourself to the success that you see all around you, it may be more beneficial to soak it up and draw from their stories for inspiration. I see Mr. Newton and your classmates are meeting at the table by the window. I'll excuse myself and let you join them. If you need anything, I'll be back in the morning. Oh, and Willa, have fun!"

Willa sits in the open seat next to Mr. Newton, noticing he changed into a pressed chambray button-down shirt for dinner. She hadn't thought about changing her clothes after fending for her life. She places her notebook and pen on the table before her and fiddles with sea glass like a worry stone until the rest of the group is ready to share their work.

Of course, Mitchell is the first to volunteer, but his story of learning to drive isn't very compelling. To create a safe space for sharing, Mr. Newton asks us to refrain from commenting on each other's stories. This initial assignment aims to explore our willingness to reveal something about ourselves that evokes an emotional response. Audrey wrote about not measuring up to her brother, who went on to get his law degree, and how her parents always favored him. Rajat shared his story about moving from India to America and the challenges he faced in obtaining citizenship. It fascinated her to learn that the four of them came from entirely different backgrounds.

"Alright, we are ready to hear from you, Willa," says Mr. Newton.

Willa placed sea glass in front of her and began to read: "My six-year-old body was spotted with red dye and mercury. In fact, my mother told me I looked like a leper, the one I learned about in Sunday School. My parents were embarrassed to take me to public places because I had clawed the mosquito bites raw on every limb of my body. Their attempt to keep me from scratching was to pour Merthiolate over my open wounds, which burned, rather than protecting me from getting bitten in the first place. I was told to be ashamed of my appearance, but at the age of six, I didn't know how to relieve the itch without scratching. Every summer for many years, I wore the coat of a leper. My God, I have scars, not tattoos." Willa pauses before saying, "I'm sorry, I should've written something else to share. But I just got eaten alive by mosquitoes at the picnic table outside, and it brought back all those memories." She closes her notebook, tucking sea glass into her pocket, and excuses herself from the meeting.

PULSE

Can you imagine what it would sound like to silence everything except heartbeats and have them amplified?

—*My Embrace*, by Lori Joseph

30

WILLA

The temperature in Willa's cabin drops significantly overnight, so she gets up to close the windows and can't fall back asleep. She tosses and turns because her stomach is growling with hunger. After excusing herself from last night's meeting, she was too embarrassed to join the group for dinner. Thank God for the welcome basket of goodies, Willa thinks as she digs in to find pretzels, a bag of Cajun snack mix, a Gala apple, some chocolates, and a note card.

Dear O'Keefe Cabin Guest(s),

Breakfast will be delivered to your cabin by 7 a.m. daily. Please place your breakfast basket on the porch when you depart for your morning class. This will ensure that guests' baskets are refilled. Additional snacks and drinks are available for purchase in the main lodge on an honor system.

Enjoy your stay at the McGrady Colony!

Sophie Halloway

Checking the time, Willa opts to eat the apple to take the edge off. She decides to shower to get ready for the day, hoping breakfast will soon be there and offer something more substantial to eat.

She sits down to write about her stay at the colony when there's a sudden rap on her cabin door. Willa crosses the room and opens the door but sees no one. She looks down at her feet to see the Breakfast Fairy has left a basket.

Eager to delve in, Willa pulls on the linen napkin to find a warm, freshly baked Morning Glory muffin, butter and jam, scrambled eggs, crispy bacon, and a mixed fruit cup. She sits in the Adirondack chair on the porch to enjoy her breakfast. She's grateful to have this experience, even though yesterday's reading left her feeling vulnerable. Today, she feels more confident with her good luck charm in her shirt pocket and wearing her favorite cowboy boots. Finished and satisfied with breakfast, Willa goes to the main lodge for the first session. Mr. Newton is already sitting in the library and motions for her to join him.

"Good morning!" says Mr. Newton.

"Good morning, Mr. Newton," Willa gives him a smile.

"Please, call me Robert. We prefer to keep things on a first-name basis around here. We missed you at dinner last night."

"I guess I didn't feel very hungry after …" Willa's focus suddenly blurred.

"After sharing your writing?" Robert asks knowingly.

Willa nods, unable to look at him.

"You did exactly what I asked you to do. It was a solid effort. Not only did your writing elicit a response from your peers, but it also got my attention. As writers, it's essential for us to go beyond the surface of our emotions to get to the good stuff—the gold."

"Is it normal to perspire or sweat when writing?" Willa asks. "I've even found myself crying out loud."

Robert raises and cants his head, saying nothing but giving her a smiling nod. He taps his fingers on the arm of the worn leather chair he is sitting in and let his gaze fall down to Willa's boots. "Nice boots!"

"Thank you. I like how I feel when I wear boots. Plus, I'm two inches taller."

Noticing Robert is wearing a pair of docksiders, Willa asks, "Have you ever tried wearing a pair of boots?"

"No, I haven't, but I can appreciate the details and craftsmanship."

"Speaking of craftsmanship, I noticed your walking stick; it's made of hickory, isn't it?"

"Indeed, it is," Robert said, handing it to her for a closer look.

Willa asks, "Do the notches reflect the trails you've hiked?"

"No, actually, they represent the number of stories I've written and published. The smaller notches are for short stories, and the longer ones are for essays." Robert replied.

"WOW, that's impressive. The notches create quite an interesting pattern. What do the rings signify?" Willa asks as she surveys the stick.

"Those are the number of films and documentaries I've produced." He tells her.

Filled with curiosity, Willa asks, "What about the gemstone inlay on top? What does it signify?"

Appreciating her interest, Robert said, "The amethyst was a gift I received from someone dear to me." He pauses to clear his throat while tugging to straighten the herringbone vest he's wearing over a classic tattersall shirt with the cuffs rolled up.

Willa notices a small verse tattooed on his forearm but can't read it from her vantage point.

Looking over Willa's shoulder, he spoke, "I thought it would be a good idea to have it be part of my history, along with my stories."

"It's such a beautiful color." Willa closes her eyes as she runs her fingers across the gemstone, sensing there is far more to be told in this moment of silence.

"Good morning, you two!" Sophie's abrupt entrance startled them from their thoughts.

"Good morning, Sophie," they respond in unison.

"Willa, I have some paperwork that you still need to complete. The pages must have gotten stuck together. I see the rest of your class is coming in the door to get started. Can you please come see me before lunch? It'll only take a few minutes."

"Sure."

"Great. See you soon!" Sophie said as she left the library.

31

WILLA

Good morning," Robert announces. "This morning I'd like you to consider the many books you've read and those that have become your favorites. What is it about those books that resonates with you, and why? I'd like you to select three of your favorites and take a few minutes to jot down what these books have in common. This exercise in discovery will lend itself to improving your style of writing.

"Once you're done, I would like you to compare those findings with what you read to the group last night. Does your writing reflect the same passion and imagery of the writers that you value? If not, take another stab at it. Think about how your treasured authors would write your story."

Willa looks up to meet Mr. Newton's eyes. Feeling his unspoken encouragement, she opens her notebook to try again.

"You can stay here to write in the library, or you're welcome to use the grounds. Let your intuition lead the way. After lunch, we'll reconvene in the Gardens where we met yesterday." Says Robert.

After several failed attempts, Willa decides to go for a walk, stopping at Sophie's desk on her way out.

"Hi Sophie, I came to fill out the rest of the paperwork."

"Perfect, she says, handing Willa a clipboard. How was your first night's stay?"

"I am in love with the O'Keefe Cabin. I feel a deep nostalgia for those who have stayed there before me. It's fun to read their comments in the Guestbook. This morning, the Breakfast Fairies even delivered an amazing basket of food to my door."

"Another magical gift of the Colony." Says Sophie.

Completing the paperwork, Willa sets the clipboard on Sophie's desk.

"Remind me, does your cottage have a back porch that overlooks the river?"

"It sure does. I'm going there now to work on my assignment." The sound of Willa walking on the wooden floor catches Sophie's attention.

"Where did you get those boots?" Sophie stands to get a better look at them.

Willa turns back to Sophie, "Oh, I've had these for a couple of years; I bought them before I left Nebraska."

"Oh my gosh, I lived in Nebraska for a few years. That's where I became obsessed with cowboy boots. Where in Nebraska?"

"Sidney, it's a small town on the western side of the state. I was born and raised there."

"That's where I lived!"

"Well, you are the first person I've met that knows of Sidney."

They went on to chat about the nuances of living there, talking about the extreme winds and temperature shifts, how to occasionally time it right to get around the trains from one end of town to the other, and how they miss the big skies and openness. Sophie recalls walking Pence along the Lodgepole Trail, to which Willa laughs and says her parents used to take her to ride her tricycle on the trail.

"My kids must have been ahead of you in school. What a small world." Sophie said.

"It's been great connecting with you, Sophie. I wish we could chat longer, but I need to get this assignment done."

"Of course, I understand." Feeling an energetic ping of connection with Willa, Sophie hopes they will have the chance to visit again.

Talking with Sophie about Sidney unexpectedly causes Willa to feel a little homesick for the familiar.

32

SOPHIE

Sophie returns home from work and turns on some music. Bonnie Raitt's version of Angel from Montgomery fills the cottage. It's a good day. She sings along, opening windows for fresh air. Thinking of her conversation with Willa and how crazy it was to meet someone from the same town she had once lived in. She steps outside to get her mail to find a small package from England in her mailbox. Inside, the note reads:

Dear Mom,

We were traipsing around some antique stores today and thought of you. You've been through a lot of changes, and now, with Pence gone, we thought you could use something to lift your spirits.

Remember the sea glass you found at the beach? We know how much it means to you, and when we stumbled upon this little bottle, the color of it instantly reminded us of that day. Maybe you could keep some of Pence's ashes in the bottle.

We're doing well and are beginning to make friends in the neighborhood. Our flat is finally starting to feel like home, but we could sure use your touch with decorating. Hopefully, you will be able to visit us soon.

Dad has kept in communication with us via occasional phone calls, but his voice sounds different now, more distant. I can't explain it, but it's got to be a massive adjustment for the both of you to pick up your lives after divorce.

It's great to hear that your new job is going well and that you're back in New England. We think the area suits you perfectly.

Keep us posted on your continued journey, and we will do the same.

OXOX Isla and Will

Sophie opens the bubble-wrapped gift to discover a little antique bottle painted with gold accents. She unscrews the lid to find there is no longer a trace of its contents, but holding it in her hands brings on a surge of happy tears. What a thoughtful gift. Sophie wants to call them right away to thank them, but when she looks at the time, she knows it is too late to call. They'd be asleep.

She sets the bottle on the mantle next to the wooden box containing Pence's ashes. Behind them is the antique mirror she purchased years ago at a tag sale. Staring at her teary reflection, Sophie hears the song 'Landslide' by Fleetwood Mac playing in the background and realizes how relevant the lyrics are to her in that moment.

Pouring herself a glass of Cabernet, she sits down and decides to search the internet for the history of the little bottle. She discovers it was made of Opaline during the 1800s, was often made in France or Italy, and was used to hold perfume.

The kids were right; the color looks just like the color of the sea glass she found on the beach in Ogunquit. To imagine the possibility of a little perfume bottle's remnants making its way to the beaches of Maine was incredible.

33

SOPHIE

It's 3:30 a.m. when Sophie wakes up on the couch. She is chilled from the night air and the dream she just had. She grabs her journal to record her thoughts from the dream, or was it a vision?

There was an elderly woman on a ship from the past. There were lots of people onboard, and they were dressed in drab colors, which she thought was reminiscent of sometime in the early 1800s. The seas were rough, and the sails were tattered. Many appeared famished and ill. Holding onto the rail with one hand, the elderly woman struggles to keep her footing. She manages to take a small bottle of perfume from her satchel to inhale its scent. She saw me watching and offered it to me. Her eyes were a cloudy gray color, matching her complexion. The earthy fragrance provided momentary relief from the stench around us. As I was about to hand it back to her, the ship was struck by a wave, sending the bottle in my hand and many screaming passengers overboard. The woman vanished, too. I was hanging onto the rail with both hands when we were hit with another wave, causing the main mast to topple. Drenched to the bones, I could see land in the distance but doubted... I would ever step foot upon it.

Sophie guardedly looks at the bottle, the gift, on the mantle. It was as if she had just been shown the origin of the sea glass, the piece she had found years earlier. She has never before considered she was part of its history, but that's got her thinking about the energy imbued in everything around her. Whether it's natural or man-made, she has always believed there is a connection to everything that exists.

Pacing the floor in a state of ambivalence, Sophie pulls on a sweater to rid herself of goosebumps and makes a cup of chamomile tea to calm her nerves. What would she do with this information?

34

WILLA

Writing on the back porch, overlooking the stream, proves beneficial for Willa. She rewrites her story using the theory of omission technique. Her revision succinctly reads: Every summer for many years, I wore the coat of a leper. My God, I have scars, not tattoos.

Arriving at the Gardens, Willa notices the plants flourished overnight. There are loads of new blossoms with ambitious bees to collect their nectar.

When it's her turn, Willa stands to share her rewrite with the class. She watches as her classmates recognize the impact of fewer words. Ultimately leaving them to conjure their own interpretation. Roberts' applause causes Willa to flush, knowing she earned his approval.

Later that evening, Sophie's words, "You have every right to be here," echo in Willa's mind as she prepares to join the group for dinner.

Willa enters the main lodge to hear Pachelbel's Canon D Major being played by two of the student musicians. The music electrifies the lodge like fireflies in a meadow. Willa is holding sea glass in her hand as she enters the dining room, where a wall of windows overlooks the gardens, dappled with solar lights. The tables are dressed with white linens and vases filled with fresh flowers grown on the property. The colorful pottery vases and batiked napkins, made by previous colony attendees, add to the vibrant scene where tonight they are encouraged to dine with those from different artistic mediums.

Filled with wonderment, Willa can't imagine her experience getting any better when she hears Sophie call her name.

"Come sit with us," Sophie calls, patting the seat next to her to complete their table of eight.

Willa discreetly tucks the sea glass into her purse and sits down next to Sophie, with Robert flanking Sophie's right. The food is served family-style, and with each passing, someone shares their name, field of study, and where they are from.

When it's Willa's turn, Sophie announces to the group that she and Willa share Nebraska roots, which leads to a lot of questions and conversation about how Willa ended up in Maine. During the meal, Willa enjoys learning about their paths to find some of them felt the same way she did about whether or not they deserved to attend such a life-changing workshop.

Robert listens intently before proposing a toast while an assortment of sumptuous pies are being served for dessert. "I have had the good fortune of being part of this amazing Colony for nearly three decades. It is our pleasure to invite you here and to witness your growth. As an artist, it is your job to reveal what others ignore. To confront what is essential by telling the story that already exists within you. Hold your glasses high, your intentions pure; Salute! Everyone clinked their glasses together in celebration.

"What a terrific evening!" Willa exclaims to Sophie and Robert as everyone was departing the dining room. "I feel so privileged to have had this opportunity. It's a far cry from Community College, but it's really great to know this Colony exists."

"Willa, you know where to reach me if you ever want to talk shop." Robert offers.

"Thank you, Robert. I will take you up on that offer. Besides, I'd like to read your story about the amethyst someday. May I give you a hug?"

"Absolutely!" He welcomes their embrace.

Willa takes his hands into hers, "Robert Newton, your encouragement has given me the ability to dream, and to believe in myself."

"That's quite a compliment, Willa." Robert replied feeling honored.

Willa turns to Sophie, a little teary-eyed, "May I hug you too?"

"Of course you can. I feel like we are boot-loving kindred spirits." Sophie shared.

"Let's keep in touch. I'd love for you to come visit me in Maine."

Feeling like they had met an old soul, Sophie and Robert looked on as the sound of Willa's footsteps in those cowboy boots faded into the night as she left the hall.

"Sometimes, it's tough to let the fledglings go." Robert said, tapping his walking stick on the floor.

"Robert, I didn't take you to be that sentimental guy." Sophie took hold of his arm as they walked to their cars.

35

WILLA

While driving back to Maine from the workshop, Willa reflects on how much her life has changed since leaving Nebraska. The friends she's making are a diverse group, and the absence of pettiness and self-absorption from classmates in high school is a welcome improvement. Conversations with Professor Malicoat, Tilghman, Sophie, and Robert have all been enjoyable yet distinct, which she attributes to their age and occupation. Unlike Paul and Gilly, Willa feels at ease sharing thoughts and listening to each of them while learning to trust her instincts.

The following morning, Willa returns to her classes, excited to share her colony experience with Professor Malicoat. "I can't thank you enough for suggesting I apply to the McGrady Colony workshop. It was life-changing for me to witness so many artists gathered in one place."

"You're very welcome. I knew you would make a great candidate. When students like you come along, it gives me great pleasure to help you flourish. Most students attend community college because they aren't sure which direction they want to take to further their education, but on occasion, we happen to notice the standouts, and you are one of them."

"There was creativity everywhere I looked. I feel like I improved in just one weekend. I can only imagine what will happen over time, and Mr. Newton, I mean Robert, is fantastic. He has a very gentle, positive approach to nudging us to find our voice. The whole experience was just magical."

"Glad to hear this, Willa."

"Thanks again." Willa said, leaving Professor Malicoat's classroom.

Still on a high from the weekend, Willa returns home from classes and calls Sophie to invite her to come for a visit.

"Hello, this is Sophie."

"Hi Sophie, it's Willa."

"Hi! How can I help you? Did you leave something behind?" "

"No, I'm calling to invite you to come for a visit."

"Strike while the iron's hot, as the saying goes," Sophie said with a chuckle. "I was hoping we could get to know one another better. In all honesty, I'm feeling a little homesick and would really enjoy your company." Looking at her calendar with nothing booked on the foreseeable weekends, Sophie replies, "That's so nice of you to offer. How about the weekend after next?"

"Perfect. I have that weekend off from work. I'll email my address to you."

"Okay, great. I look forward to our visit."

"Me too!"

Later that evening, Sophie checks for Willa's email to find the address: *37 Derringer Road, Ogunquit, ME.* Ogunquit, of all places. Thinking back to the vacation she had with her family decades ago. To where she had found the Opaline sea glass on the beach.

36

SOPHIE

Preparing to leave Dublin by 7 a.m., Sophie sets her suitcase, sunglasses, and the vase she'd purchased from the Colony for Willa next to the door. Although they've just met, Willa feels like an old friend to Sophie. She hopes she's making the right choice by accepting Willa's invitation. Erin, the twelve-year-old daughter of her neighbor, is happy to come over and feed the cat while Sophie is away. The next morning, Sophie loads her car and, by habit, opens the door for Pence to hop in the back seat. In that moment, she knows she has to bring him along and goes back inside to retrieve the box from the mantle, placing it on the front seat next to her. She then heads east with her co-pilot.

The closer she gets to the ocean, the more exhilarated she feels. Why hadn't I thought of going before now? Turning the music off and opening the windows, she focuses on the weekend ahead.

The salt air smells a tad fishy from the low tide as she crosses over the bridge. Gulls are squawking and circling over the marsh grass. Sophie turns onto Derringer Road to find the plum rose and sea oats bowing over the edges of the lane when her curiosity piques. There are only four cottages perched on the dunes at the end of the cul-de-sac. She looks up to see Willa getting out of her car and pulls into the drive without having to search for house numbers.

Willa waves. "You made it! I was moving my car over so there would be room for you to park your car too."

"It was a beautiful morning for a drive. Willa, I had no idea you lived on the water. What a surprise."

"I was as surprised as you. When my Aunt Eva left me her cottage, I had no idea it was on the water until I made the trek down Derringer Road. Let me help you with your bags."

Entering the door by the kitchen, Sophie immediately sees the windows and door opposite them that overlook the ocean. "Wow, what a view. This is a fantastic location."

Pleased with her delight, Willa responds, "I'm so glad you're here. You've got the bedroom and bath upstairs."

Sophie follows her up the painted staircase, noticing the give and creaks characteristic of an old home. The bedroom is sparsely decorated but feels fresh and welcoming nonetheless. There's a small desk and some poetry books. The nightstand has a vase of fresh wildflowers with a couple of seashells sitting next to it.

"There are hangers in the armoire, extra blankets in the trunk, and the bath is across the hall. I am going to the market to pick up some things. I shouldn't be too long. Please make yourself at home. There are a couple of tea options in the cupboard and drinks in the fridge."

Willa thought it would be best to allow Sophie time alone to explore the cottage. She remembers the magic of discovery when she first stepped foot into Aunt Eva's world and wanted Sophie to experience it for herself.

Sophie walks to the window, which is propped open with a sliding screen. The linen curtains are hand-embroidered and pulled to one side, exposing a view of the beach, calling her to the water. With the same urgency her kids had years ago, she kicks her shoes off and is out the door, running onto the beach. And she keeps running, passing people flying kites, building sandcastles, and a man walking his dog. The dog's coat and markings are similar to Pence's, evoking a jolt to her emotions. She runs faster and faster, but everywhere she looks, there are reminders of the family she once had. Humiliation and anger forge a sobbing, making it hard for her to catch her breath, until she can no longer run. Sophie collapses with exhaustion, letting the waves encircle and submerge her feet.

Unaware of how long she'd sat there or how far she'd run, a flock of encroaching seagulls calls her to her feet just before a huge wave is about to make land. Soaked to her waist and thirsty, she treks to drier sand and heads back to Willa's cottage. The rhythm of the ocean is therapeutic for Sophie. It feels good to release and let go of those feelings. She thinks back to Avery's goal of helping her heal from a place of empowerment rather than being a victim. Sophie likens her latest release of emotions and feelings to journaling, realizing how cathartic it is to acknowledge her feelings and disconnect from them with compassion. Feeling proud of herself for her progress, she walks, noticing the day is getting much warmer.

A parade of people carrying umbrellas, coolers, and chairs is coming over the beach access trail when Sophie is suddenly aware that she didn't think to look back at Willa's place before taking off running. She doesn't have a clue about the color of her porch and didn't make a note of any visual features, leaving her to wonder how she will find the cottage. She does remember there are stairs, but almost every place along this beach has stairs. At least I'm headed in the right direction.

A man is hanging an OPEN flag on the porch of an ice cream shop, so she approaches him.

"Good morning," Sophie says, drenched in sweat again as she follows him into the shop.

"Good morning to you. We've just opened up for the day."

"Would it be possible to get a bottle of water? I'm embarrassed to admit that I arrived in town this morning and was so eager to take a run that I neglected to make note of the house where I'm staying. I promise to pay you for the water later. I didn't bring anything with me on my run."

He studies her for a moment with his amber eyes, reaches into the cooler behind the counter and places a bottle of water in front of her.

"Thank you so much…" Sophie said hoping he would tell her his name.

"Will. And you're welcome."

"I'm Sophie; I have a son named Will. It's a good name." Taking a long drink, Sophie says, " I'll bring my friend back for ice cream later." As she is about to walk out the door, Sophie turns and asks, "Will, do you happen to know how far it is to Derringer Road? "

"It's about two and a half miles from here. You'll see The Woodford Gallery when you're close. The owner often gives plein air classes on the beach, but if he isn't out there, just look for the shop with all the nautical flags and spinners hanging on the porch. You can't miss it; Derringer Road is probably another hundred yards beyond the gallery."

"Thanks again. I'll be back." Sophie replies while holding the bottle of cold water to her neck.

Relieved to have finally reached the gallery with all of the brightly colored flags, Sophie knows it isn't too much further. Her legs feel heavy, and her clothes are already dry. She focuses on the cottages, hoping she'll see something familiar. Up ahead, she sees Willa standing at the top of the steps, waving to her.

"Did you get lost?" Willa asks, hoping that wasn't the case.

"Oh, not really, I just took a nice long run down the beach. Farther than what I had anticipated, but it was worth it," Sophie says, quickly climbing the stairs that were scorching hot from the sun.

"Are you ready for some brunch?"

"Yes, I'm famished." Sophie said. Realizing how hungry she was.

"I made egg salad sandwiches with slices of cucumber."

"Sounds perfect." Sophie says, eager to calm the rumblings in her stomach.

Willa and Sophie grab their plates and head to the screened-in porch that overlooks the ocean.

"Be careful, that screen door sticks to the floorboard," Willa warns.

"Got it!" Sophie replies, taking in her surroundings. The porch ceiling is painted a light blue hue, mirroring the sky that day. An old swing hung with rope is tucked at the end of the porch, where tethered sailcloth curtains hang as a wind barrier. There are potted plants and baskets heaped with shells stacked on top of a lobster trap in the corner. A string of lights with fishnet holds sand dollars and small pieces of driftwood across the railing. Sophie was intrigued to see two easels with blank canvases, along with a selection of paint and brushes.

"Would you like some iced tea?" asks Willa.

"Sounds great." I think I'm still feeling a little parched from my run. "This sandwich sure looks delicious."

Willa returns with a pitcher of iced tea mixed with orange slices and fresh mint on the side.

"I was noticing the artwork on the porch. I didn't realize you painted." Sophie says after finishing a big bite of the sandwich.

"It's just a hobby." Willa states. "Do you paint or have a creative outlet?"

"I painted for fun with Will and Isla, my children, when they were little."

"Where are they now?"

"They're living in England. After they graduated from college, they decided to try living abroad. It makes sense for them to go while they are young and eager to explore the world."

"I've never traveled outside of the country, but I would like to think I might someday. I was thinking we can do some painting after we're done eating. We tried this technique in a theory class at the community college, and I thought it would be fun to share it with you."

"Okay, I'll give it a try, but I don't consider myself an artist. Are those your paintings in the house?"

"Most of them."

"They're so fun and vibrant and clearly show you have talent. I passed the Woodford Gallery on my run. Have you been there?"

"I haven't, but we should try to go while you're here."

They finish eating, and Willa clears the table to make room for the painting supplies. While in the kitchen, she checks her phone to see she's missed a call from Tilghman and realizes it makes her smile.

"This cottage is so charming. I love how you've kept the vintage look," Sophie says, bringing her plate to the sink.

"Almost everything in here was my Aunt Eva's. Keeping it is my way to honor her. We only met once when I was a little girl, so it's pretty special to know that she remembered me even though we never had the chance to get to know one another. Moving here has allowed me to learn more about her, at least the things she valued. Her collection of books and records, the spices she used in cooking, and the photographs all tell me a little more about her life story. Evidently, she was a great teacher because I've heard from numerous people how much they appreciated her at the school. Shall we go paint?" Willa grins, handing Sophie a still-warm chocolate chip cookie.

They set up on the porch, and Willa shares, "The idea of this painting exercise is meant to allow yourself to engage with your heart."

"Whoa," Sophie laughs nervously.

"Relax, it's not meant to be perfect or anything. We're supposed to think of something we wish for from our heart and write that word on the board. You won't see the word when you're done with your painting, but it is setting the intention to fulfill your wish. Trust me, the results are amazing. Our entire class was transformed by this exercise. Feel free to move or adjust your easel to any height that suits you for painting. I'm going to move mine over here to sit and look out at the water."

Sophie decides to move hers to the opposite end of the porch, facing the same direction. Contemplating her morning run and how her life has been turned upside down, she picks up the pencil and lightly writes the heartfelt word, Resilience.

"What should I do once I've written the word on my canvas?"

"You paint! There's no right or wrong way to paint. It can be realistic or abstract; it can be a color story or a wash. It's more about thinking about your word as you add color and texture to your canvas. I had classmates who started painting one thing and ended up with a completely new concept by the time they were done. Our professor just encouraged us to keep feeling and keep painting."

"How did you know when you were done?"

"Good question. We asked the same thing, and our professor was right; you'll know in your heart when it's done."

Inspired by the sky, Sophie begins painting in shades of light blue, watching her word disappear with the layers of paint. The more she painted, the more hypnotic it felt as the scent of plum rose and the ocean breeze filled her lungs. She couldn't remember the last time she had breathed so deeply. Thinking of this triggers a feeling of resentment, and with that feeling, she adds strokes of Payne's gray, forest green, navy blue, and black. It's startling to see the dark stripes take over the pretty blue, and Sophie recognizes she needs to shift her focus. While those layers of paint are drying, she thinks of the bottle Isla and Will sent her, conjuring memories of their trip to Ogunquit. She selects a broad brush and starts adding metallic gold, dry-brushing it in a cross-hatched pattern over the board. Sophie is so into the moment that she doesn't notice

Willa has stepped away until she overhears her talking to someone.

"Hi Tilghman, I got your message. I appreciate the offer. Is my rain check still good?"

"Yes, of course." Says Tilghman.

"I have a friend visiting this weekend. In fact, we're spending the afternoon out on the porch."

"Are you on the porch now?"

"No, I stepped inside to return your call."

"Go out on your porch and look straight out."

Willa looks out onto the beach, searching for Tilghman. "I don't see you."

"I can see you."

"Wait, where are you?"

"I brought the Sun Dog out for the afternoon."

Willa looks out over the water to see Tilghman waving. Excited to see him, she waves back.

"Hey, I just thought it would be fun to call you from the water. Have a good time with your friend. Talk soon."

"Okay, have fun." Willa hangs up and turns to Sophie, "Well, that was a nice surprise."

"A good one, I take it? "

Willa smiles in response, "Yes."

Sophie stands to stretch and take a break. She studies Willa's painting. It is a whimsical painting of a beach umbrella painted in shades of red on a sandy beach. So stylized yet straightforward. "What word did you write on your canvas?"

Willa laughs, "I wrote 'Love. I want to know what it feels like to be in love."

"You may already know," Sophie says with a wink, motioning to the sailboat that looks half its size from just a few minutes ago. " He looks good from here!"

Willa shrugs. "We'll see."

"I'm not done painting, but I'd like to let it sit for a while. I'm going to refill my tea, and then I want to hear all about the guy on the boat."

"There isn't too much to tell you at this point. Tilghman is the lawyer who handled my aunt's estate. He's lived here his whole life, and he likes to sail. He called to invite me to go sailing again today."

"Again? You've sailed with him before?"

"Yeah, we bumped into each other at the bakery, and he suggested I join him for a sail. Since I'd never gone before, I thought it might be fun. I'll admit I was a little nervous, but not so much about sailing."

"What were you nervous about?"

"Well...it's just that I overheard Carol, his administrative assistant, talking on the phone with someone I have reason to believe may be involved with the human trafficking investigation that's happening in town. The whole thing creeps me out."

"Does Tilghman know you overheard the conversation?"

"No. It happened right before we were to meet at the marina, so it felt weird to cancel at the last minute. We had a really nice time getting to know one another. Deep down, I'm really hoping he isn't involved or representing someone like Gilly or Paul. If he is, I don't want anything to do with him."

"Who's Gilly and Paul?"

Willa pauses before responding, and Sophie senses a marked uneasiness in her voice. "Let's just say they are adult men behaving badly, and it won't surprise me if they are found guilty. They are restaurateurs who have a reputation for taking advantage of their staff, but I didn't know any of this before I started working for them. I got out as fast as I could and started working for Avery. She owns the hardware store in town."

Sophie hugs Willa to comfort her and says, "I'm sorry you had to deal with such slugs. You deserve to know what it feels like to be in love."

"Now that I've spilled, tell me something about you." Says Willa.

"You and I have a connection," Sophie says and begins to pace the floor, considering how much of her story she's willing to share with Willa. Not wanting to discourage Willa's quest for love, she opts to give an abbreviated version of the story.

"I was married to Eric for over twenty-five years, and we enjoyed a lot of good times together, but, as clichéd as it sounds, our marriage ran its course. That's behind me now, but here's a fun fact: our family vacationed in Ogunquit many years ago."

"Really? Was that before or after you lived in Nebraska?" "

"Long before. Our kids were only four and six at the time. I loved bringing them to the ocean because I got as much enjoyment out of it as they did. We used to love playing in the sand and walking along a trail from the beach to get ice cream. Which reminds me, we need to go visit Will, the ice cream man. I promised him I would come back to pay for my water."

Willa looks at her questioningly, but Sophie wasn't prepared to let Willa in on her emotional release marathon, so she passes it off by responding, "I got a little too ambitious on my run this morning and really needed a drink of water." It just so happened that Will was putting up the "Open for Business" flag at the same time I was passing by his shop. He's got dreamy amber eyes. Oh, but he's way too old for you." Sophie said, jokingly. "What do you say we freshen up and catch dinner somewhere nearby? My treat. I'd like you to pick the restaurant since you know the ones we should avoid, and then we can stop over at Will's to get an ice cream for dessert."

37

SOPHIE

Sophie wakes up in the middle of the night to find her T-shirt is soaked with perspiration. The chain on the whirling ceiling fan above her randomly clinks against the light shade and is impossible to ignore. She changes into a loose-fitting sleeveless shirt dress and tiptoes downstairs. The whitecaps glow in the moonlight while she stands listening to the incoming tide pound the surf. Before long, her breath is in rhythm with the sea, connecting her to this place in her heart. She turns on the little string lights on the porch, picks up a brush from earlier, and begins painting over the dark layers and metallic gold, as if the ocean is guiding her in choosing the colors. Alternating brushes from white to shades of turquoise, she strokes in a repetitive trance. Wiping away some of the paint to allow the gold to show through and adding darker turquoise for depth. Time lapsed with the tide before she steps back to evaluate her painting. Sophie knows she is finished, but she never expected to see the resemblance to the Opaline bottle.

Beyond the porch, silhouetted figures are scattered across the beach in the twilight. For Sophie, it is a moment of reverence before the sun rises for another day.

"Good morning," Willa quietly says, handing Sophie a cup of tea.

"Thanks," says Sophie. "You're up early, too."

"Yeah, I tend to wake up with the birds."

While watching the morning unfold, they sit in silence, allowing the tea to steep in their mugs. Willa looks over to notice Sophie has closed her eyes as if she's in a meditative state. Taking in a deep breath herself, she feels grateful to share this new day with her new friend. Minute by minute, the colors in the sky begin to show the promise of the sun's return while the tide inches further away. The beach is coming alive with people, and before either of them speak, the sun makes its debut. Illuminating everything and everybody in its path.

"What an amazing way to greet the day," Sophie says while removing the steeper ball from her tea. "This tea smells wonderful."

"It's an Indian chai blend, one of my favorites." Says Willa, offering Sophie some milk.

"I can taste the cardamom and chicory; it's very flavorful. I don't know that I've ever had anything quite like it."

"It's like a hug in a mug," Willa says, and they chuckle.

Staring out over the water, Sophie says, "It never gets old. It's like a surprise gift each morning with different colors in the sky, clouds, and no clouds. Isn't it something that, no matter what's happening in the world, we can count on this every day?"

"It feels pretty special to me, too. Speaking of which, thank you for dinner last night; I've been wanting to try that place, but never really wanted to go by myself. It's good to know they offer a takeout menu."

"They were hopping busy. I've never been to a place where you can bring your own wine and food to add to their menu offerings. Did you notice a family brought their own linens and candles for the table?" Sophie asks.

"I did, and they were celebrating with champagne. It would be a great place to host a small party, even though there's a two-hour time limit. Sophie, I picked up some pastries for us yesterday morning; let me get those, and I'll be right back. Would you like a warmer for your tea?" Willa asks.

"Yes, please."

Willa returns and sets the small tray of goodies on the table when Sophie's painting catches her eye. "Sophie, it's beautiful! When did you finish your painting?"

"I came downstairs during the night, and the moonlight was so bright it looked as though the waves were illuminated. Their colors inspired me, and I was drawn back to the easel."

"Do you love it?"

"I do. Mainly because you introduced me to the technique. I had no idea when I wrote the word 'resilience' that I would experience such emotional and transformative shifts while painting. I went from feeling inadequate to some really low places and feeling angry. I didn't like how that made me feel, so I had to search for something to be grateful for. I thought of the kindness Will extended to me by giving me a bottle of water when I was parched from running. This probably sounds crazy, but his eyes had gold highlights in them, so I added his kindness, his gold, to my painting."

"It doesn't sound crazy to me at all. Our connection and the one you had with the Ice Cream Man, in my mind, validate the idea that we are all connected to one another. The turquoise color in your painting even reminds me of my good luck charm."

"Really, you have a talisman?"

"Yes. I've had it since I was a little girl and have carried it in my pocket for years. I found it at the Goodwill Store in Sidney. Did you ever go there?"

"Only to drop off donations."

"I loved going there and browsing through all the donated items. I think Sidney was unique in having a big business with its world headquarters in such a small town. Employees were recruited from everywhere, and when they'd move to town for work, they'd bring and eventually donate clothes and treasures collected from around the world.

"I remember the day I found my good luck charm as if it were yesterday. It was sitting in a glass jar at eye level when I walked down the aisle. I'd never seen anything like it. I had to have it."

"Can I see it?"

"Sure, it's on my nightstand, I'll go get it."

Willa returns, handing the sea glass to Sophie, "Look how similar its color is to your painting."

38

SEA GLASS

After all these years, I wasn't sure how I would feel resting in Sophie's hands again. So much has changed, and yet it feels like this is the path we are destined to take. We were together for many years until we weren't, just like she and Eric. Sophie's fear and unwillingness to honor her truth and her instincts created such turmoil within that it caused her to emotionally disengage. It was hard for me to witness and even harder to be cast aside. I kept wanting to believe we were meant to be together. Feeling abandoned, I held onto a belief that I created rather than accepting that there could be greater opportunities for both of us.

I never imagined the faceted jelly jar she put me in would ultimately save me, but it did. My perspective changed and developed while I was in the jar at the Goodwill Store. As I watched other castoffs come and go, my curiosity grew, softening my anger and resentment. I discovered that when I focused on finding something good, even if it was a tiny prism of light, I started to feel at peace within. My gratitude grew a little each day, and I became an example of the law of attraction. Willa was just a little girl filled with wonderment when she discovered me. She has an astounding willingness to believe in life's possibilities. If you don't believe me, look around. Here we are at the ocean she had once dreamed of visiting after discovering me.

39

SOPHIE & WILLA

Sophie clasps the sea glass with both hands, resting her chin on them as she bows her head in search of what she might say to Willa.

"Do you feel the magic?" Willa asks, keenly focused on Sophie.

"I'm in awe," Sophie replies, taking a deep breath. "I need to tell you something."

"I'm listening."

Sophie hands the sea glass back to Willa, who sets it next to her cup of tea. "Do you remember when I told you that our family vacationed in Ogunquit years ago?"

Willa nods.

"We were on our walk back from getting ice cream when I suddenly felt the need to leave the trail and go down to the water. There was a massive piece of driftwood surrounded by tide pools. A good place to search for shells and crabs. Anyway, something caught my eye; it was partially buried in the sand." Sophie gazes at the sea glass, pausing to consider precisely what she needed to say.

Filled with realization, Willa touches the sea glass and asks, "Are you telling me you are the one who found this... my lucky charm?"

"As crazy as it sounds, yes, and I donated it to the Goodwill store in Sidney on my way out of town."

"But why didn't you keep it?" Willa asked.

"I kept it for a very long time, but when my marriage ended, I felt as though my luck had run out, so I put it in the donation box. It's incredible to think it's found its way back to Ogunquit!" Sophie exclaimed while grasping the hair on her head. "Willa, you don't suppose our friendship is an accident?"

"Not for a minute. How could it be? You and I've clicked from the moment we met. I never imagined I'd have a home in Maine, attend a writer's workshop, or sail the ocean. This is unbelievable." Shaken with the news, Willa stands to give Sophie a hug.

Sophie holds onto her new friend and says, "I never dreamed of seeing that piece of sea glass again, and now to consider how this has all happened, just blows my mind."

40

SEA GLASS

I was given a purpose when I became a perfume bottle. The fragrance also served a purpose. The people who inhaled or dabbed it onto their bodies were enlivened by hints of juniper, honey, cedar, and rose. Each fragrant note contributed in its own unique way. Like the bottle, whole or not, in time we discover our mutable purpose, our value.

As I sit here next to Willa's cup of tea, I can hear the ocean. Its repetitive movement pulses like a heartbeat, transcending my thoughts beyond what Sophie and Willa already know. Although broken, I still cradle the energy from the earth's minerals and from those who crafted and carried me. That's what love does.

41

SOPHIE & WILLA

The day unfolds for Willa and Sophie, and they take a long walk along the ocean to process their discovery and chat about life's mysteries. Willa opens up to Sophie, trusting her with the stories of her experiences at the restaurants. It feels good for Willa to finally share them with someone.

A good listener, Sophie understands why Willa couldn't go to the police for help. "You mentioned that you saw an FBI agent at the café. Do you think you can talk with him?"

"I didn't get his name, and who knows why he's in town. It may not have anything to do with the human trafficking investigation. I just thought it was weird how I got chills reading the headline and seeing him in that instant."

"I think it's remarkable that you've been able to support yourself and continue your education by working at the hardware store. You're a strong young lady."

"Thank you."

"I've really enjoyed our time together and look forward to sharing more, but I should gather my things and get on the road."

"I understand. Sophie. You're always welcome to come back."

"I would love to."

Sophie's packing her car to leave and realizes, with the excitement of her arrival, she forgot to give Willa the vase. She also has to go back upstairs to grab Pence's Box to place her co-pilot in the seat next to her for the ride home.

"Here, I brought you a small hostess gift. It's a reminder of your time at the Colony and where we first met."

"I love it," Willa says, giving Sophie a hug. "I'm going to set it on my table where I can see it every day."

"I'm so happy you like it," Sophie responds.

Willa looks around the cottage to see if there is anything else that belongs to Sophie when she spies the painting on the porch. Sophie's at the base of the stairs with the box in her hands when Willa calls from the porch, "Sophie, you can't forget your painting."

"I know exactly where I'm going to hang it when I get home."

42

WILLA

Avery arrives early Monday morning to open the hardware store. Whenever she takes time off, there are always scheduling changes, paperwork, and bank deposits to catch up on. She is pleased to see that the shelves are stocked and the deliveries have been checked in by Willa. She values Willa's work ethic and accountability, but can only afford to pay her to work peak hours when the store is most busy.

While in her office, Avery hears the bell ring at the front entrance. She walks out to meet an official-looking man dressed in black that she doesn't recognize.

"Good morning. How can I help you?"

"Good morning. I'm Agent Puckett, he says, flashing his FBI badge. I'm here to speak with one of your employees, Willa Jessop."

"Willa isn't scheduled to work for another twenty minutes."

"Do you have someplace where I can wait?"

"Sure, you can use my office." Avery shows him into her office and moves some boxes and paperwork from the extra chair. "I'd offer you a coffee, but I don't have any made. There's a cooler of drinks up front. Can I get you some water?"

"That would be great. Thanks."

Avery returns, handing him the water, "May I ask what this is about?"

"I've been assigned to investigate the local human trafficking case that's been in the news. Willa worked at a couple of the restaurants accused, so I'm checking with the list of employees to see if I can get any additional information. I appreciate you letting me wait here in your office."

"Of course," Avery replies, somewhat rattled, shuffling papers on her desk.

"What do you know about Willa Jessop?"

"She's a good worker. Dependable. She started working here several months ago and has always been punctual. Willa has excellent attention to detail and always goes the extra mile to help me and our customers.

"She relocated here from Nebraska to attend the community college."

Perplexed, Agent Puckett remarked, "That's a long way from home."

"It is, but her Aunt left her estate to Willa, so that's why she's moved here."

"I see."

The bell rings again.

"I bet that's Willa," Avery leaves the office to check. "Hi, Willa."

"Good morning."

"Good to see you. Willa, there is an FBI agent in my office. He'd like to speak with you."

Willa stiffened, "Me?"

"Yes, he's been waiting for a little while. I'm sure it's probably some routine questioning. Go ahead and punch in while you're in the office. I'll cover the register."

Willa enters the office, punches in on the time clock, and sets her sandwich from the bakery on the table in front of her.

"You must be Ms. Jessop?"

"I am," she replies, looking at him with recognition.

"I'm Agent Puckett. I'm sorry to bother you at work, but I'd like to ask you a few questions."

"Okay," Willa replies, feeling apprehensive.

"Are you aware of the local human trafficking investigation happening?"

"Yes, I've read about it—well, actually, I've only read the headline in the newspaper. A few weeks ago, I caught your paper from blowing away at the bakery."

"Oh yeah, I thought you looked familiar. That's a really good bakery," Puckett says, putting her at ease.

"It's one of my favorite places in Ogunquit."

"Willa, we are asking anyone who's worked for Paul Blanchard or Gilly Owens to provide us with any information they may have that could help our investigation. What can you tell me from your experience?"

"Well, I didn't work for Paul for very long before he started hitting on me."

"Hitting you?"

"No, flirting with me. It made me really uncomfortable. He's got to be in his forties," Willa said, rolling her eyes.

"Did he flirt with other employees?"

"All the time. Paul kept suggesting they could work at one of his motels on the East Coast and make a killing."

"Did you happen to catch the name of any of those motels? "

"No, I'm sorry."

"That's okay. How did your co-workers respond?"

"Some of the girls flirted with him, but there was this one girl who I regularly saw straightening her dress as the two of them would come out of the walk-in cooler together."

"Do you think they were doing something inappropriate?"

"Absolutely. Speaking of inappropriate, Paul scheduled me to close one night. It was just the two of us there, and he approached me and told me that I should consider becoming a prostitute."

"Did he physically touch you?" Puckett asks.

"No," she says, looking him in the eye. "But it creeped me out so much that I never went back to work."

"Willa, you did the right thing by leaving. Tell me about working for Gilly." He continued with his questioning, turning the page to take more notes.

Willa shifted in her chair and dropped her focus to the bagged sandwich in front of her. "Gilly kept wanting me to go for a ride in his Corvette. I kept telling him no, but he kept asking. My gut told me he had an ulterior motive. I didn't think it would be safe to go somewhere with him in his car. I thought we came to an understanding because he stopped asking me daily. Turns out he was preying on the new girl. When I asked for a weekend off, Gilly let me take it. Unbeknownst to me at the time, he had me followed and set me up so I would think he was my hero. "

"How so?" The Agent quizzed.

"After he gave me the weekend off, I went into work the following Monday. Gilly asked me about my weekend. I told him what had happened, and he hugged me, saying he'd talk with his uncle, who's a cop, and see if they could do something to help me out.

Before the end of my shift, Gilly handed me my paycheck and said his uncle was going to stop by and would accept my check as payment to have Rich's citation cleared from the records."

"Who's Rich? He asks.

"He's my friend from college. He was going to show me around the area that weekend, before he moved out of state."

Willa goes on to tell Agent Puckett all of the details. She watches him raise an eyebrow when she shares she'd witnessed the cop dealing drugs on the delivery dock.

"Ms. Jessop, you've been very helpful. Is there anything else you can think of?"

Willa's phone pings. It's a text message from Tilghman. Thinking of him, she hesitantly asks, "Besides the restaurants, are there other businesses involved?"

"Why do you ask?"

Willa stands, patting her pocket for Sea Glass's reassurance. "I overheard Carol's phone call."

"Who's Carol?"

"She works at Graham Burkes Law Office."

"And, what else do you know about Carol?"

"She was talking to Gilly. I only know this because she was in here buying some light bulbs, and I saw his name appear on her phone. She answered his call and left in such a hurry that I ran after her to give her the change, and she was in a heated conversation with him."

"Do you remember what she said?"

"I do. She was really mad, and she said, 'Gilly, if the FBI comes knocking on my door, I won't protect you again.'"

Agent Puckett flips his notebook to a fresh page. "Is that all?"

"That's it."

"Does she know you overheard her conversation?"

"I'm pretty sure she does."

"You've given me some good intel. Here's my card. If you recall anything else, please don't hesitate to call me. Enjoy the sandwich," he says as he shakes her hand to leave.

"Thanks for your time," he says to Avery as he leaves the store.

Willa joins Avery at the register.

"Are you okay?" Avery asks.

"Yeah, he just wanted some information about the restaurants where I used to work." Willa refrained from going into detail with her.

"You seem a little shaken. Do you want to take the day off?" Avery offers.

"No, I'm fine. Besides, it's better for me to keep busy." Willa says, picking up the pricing gun to ticket some new inventory.

43

SOPHIE

McGrady Colony, this is Sophie."

A foreign voice announces, "This is Mr. Bauman; how do you do?"

"Very well, Mr. Bauman, and you?"

"I am fine, thank you. I have registered for the workshop and thought perhaps you could answer a few of my questions?" Intrigued by his accent, Sophie finds herself smiling in response, "Of course, I will certainly try to answer your concerns, Mr. Bauman."

"I wonder if you know of any places nearby where there is live music? You see, music inspires me, and I sometimes like to listen so that I can later find the words to write. Makes sense?"

"Yes, I understand. I can think of a few places in town that you may find interesting. I'll have a list of them for you when you arrive."

"Wonderful! And do you happen to know which cabin is next to the water? I'd very much like to request that one for my stay. Only, if it is not an imposition," he says, engagingly.

"The O'Keefe Cabin is on the river, but there is a hold on it. Would you like me to see if it might become available and get back to you?"

"Ah, yes, let's see, I should give you my US number as I will be arriving there in two days. You can leave a message on that line."

Sophie is lost in thought from the lilt of his voice. He will be arriving in the US in two days. Who is this man who travels from another country to attend a McGrady Colony workshop, and why am I feeling this dire need to meet him?

"Hello? Sophie?"

"Oh, oh yes, sorry, Mr. Bauman," Sophie recovers nicely, stating she is searching for a pen, which happens to be in her hand! She records and verifies his US number. "I will message you later this afternoon."

"Thank you, Sophie, I appreciate your time."

"You're very welcome. See you soon."

Sophie looks to see that it is already 11:45; she leaves the office and arrives right on time to meet with Alisha, who is waiting outside her office to go for their walk.

"Good to see you. If I didn't know any better, I'd say you have a bit of a bounce in your step today," Alisha says, noticing a shift in Sophie's energy.

"Good to see you too. It's been an eventful three weeks, and I don't even know where to begin."

"I'm intrigued." Alisha smiles. "Have you made progress with your meditation and journaling?"

"You'll be pleased to know that I am up to fifteen minutes a day and writing a lot more, but, ironically, it has nothing to do with my divorce. My children sent me a very thoughtful gift. Ever since I received it, I've been having vivid dreams and visions, so I started recording them in my journal. It's becoming quite the story. I'm excited to go to bed each night to see what comes next."

Alisha remarks, "That sounds like a very special gift."

"I'm going to try to make this brief," Sophie says to Alisha, wanting to fill her in. "I went to visit Willa, a new friend I met at the Colony, who also used to live in Nebraska. She invited me to her place in Maine, and it was in the exact town where my family vacationed." Speaking excitedly and breathless, "To top things off, when I left Nebraska, I donated a piece of sea glass to Goodwill. It was my lucky charm until it wasn't. I wasn't feeling too lucky going through the divorce. Anyway, Willa and I were chatting about talismans when she showed me her lucky charm." Sophie stops in her tracks and turns to Alisha, throwing her hands in the air as she tells her, "It is the sea glass that I found in Ogunquit. Can you believe it? And Willa has been carrying it with her for nearly a decade!"

"Really!" Alisha sounds pleased and nods.

Astounded, Sophie tells Alisha," It's as if we were meant to meet one another."

"Do you believe there's no such thing as coincidence?" Alisha asks.

"I do now!" Sophie speaks enthusiastically, "Life feels more intentional than coincidental." Sophie hurries to take a few steps ahead of Alisha, standing to face her. "Imagine being on a path or a journey, and unbeknownst to you, there are stations ahead of you where you're provided with exactly what you need. You may think I'm crazy, but recognizing this concept feels like a huge weight has been lifted from my shoulders. Everything is falling into place for me, and I think I finally know what it feels like to be in the flow."

Thrilled for Sophie, Alisha responds, "It's like tuning a radio station. When you want to hear a certain type of music or the news, you simply turn the station to the frequency you desire. You can't see it, but you believe or expect it to be there. If you change to a station expecting static, you will get static. It's the same principle if you want to heal and feel better; your focus can't be dwelling on something that went wrong; you've got to change your frequency and, most importantly, believe it's possible."

"Alisha, you amaze me. I really wish I could've taught my children this idea while they were growing up."

"It's never too late. Your children will see your transformation or hear it in your voice and most likely want to try it for themselves."

"That would be phenomenal."

"Believe," Alisha knowingly says and laughs.

"I know, I know, practice makes perfect. You have to admit, I've come a long way since our first phone call."

"Yes, Sophie, you have traveled far and made many milestones."

"Speaking of traveling far, this morning I was speaking with Mr. Hans Bauman, a guest who's coming to the Colony in a couple of days. He wants to listen to live music while he's in town. Do you have any recommendations other than the Black Pearl or Harpers?"

"You might suggest he stop by the Pavilion on Camp Dillon Road; they often have drop-in sessions Wednesday through Sunday, where musicians spontaneously gather to play. It can be a lot of fun, and sometimes famous musicians drop by, too.

"Good suggestions. Thanks. It sounds like my kind of place."

"Do you have any concerns that you would like to further discuss today?"

"I believe I'm doing okay for now. It's helped that Eric has stopped calling. I've been able to put some distance between us to focus on myself."

"You're doing great, Sophie. I'd like you to continue to lengthen your meditations. Once they become a constant part of your lifestyle, it would be nice for you to do this wherever you choose. For instance, if you're a runner, you can meditate while out for a run. Gardening is also a great time to meditate, or you can do so while engaging in any activity you enjoy. This practice is invaluable, especially during times when you don't have the opportunity to sit in the quietness of your home. It's also reassuring to know we're never really alone. There are angels, or spirits, surrounding us all the time. They want us to succeed."

"Do you talk with them?"

"I do. Think of the times when you're searching for something and it suddenly appears. Or when you place a call to a friend and they say they were just thinking of you when their phone rings. We are given countless signs of communication every day, but most people aren't tuned in enough to recognize these gifts. Have fun with it. The more you acknowledge these signs, the more you'll understand we are not alone."

Their walk leads them back to Alisha's office. "Let's schedule your next visit for two months from now. If you should need to talk with me before then, just call."

"Okay, see you next time," Sophie says before she walks to her car. "And Alisha, you've been really helpful. Without being judgmental, you've helped me to focus and discover I can trust my instincts. You're a kind soul in this crazy mixed-up world. I wish there were more people like you."

Alisha smiles, "There are, and you will find them."

44

CAROL

It is pouring rain for Carol's drive to work. The driver's side wiper blade has deteriorated to the point where the rubber is split and separated, causing the wiper arm to scrape against the windshield with each swipe. It's one of the many things Gilly has promised to take care of but never did. Carol is four years younger than Gilly, yet feels like she is the one who takes care of him, even after they became adults. Her compassion for Gilly came from the realization that it could've been her, instead of him, who would struggle with addiction. But there are other hardships for Carol to face. Weary of his lies and deceit, her perseverance is tested countless times when she bails him out of jail or meets him in the Emergency Room in the late hours of the night after he's crashed another car while driving under the influence.

Initially, Gilly's incarcerations, probations, and rehab programs gave her hope. But after serving time, he is released, falters, and succumbs to alcohol, only to repeat the story. After the shock and embarrassment of his first imprisonment, those penalties weirdly gave her peace of mind, knowing he was safe in captivity and would no longer be a risk to innocent lives or himself.

What really stings are those in town who avoid her and, in some cases, have alienated her because of association. Although she is nothing like Gilly, Carol has been ostracized for his actions, making it difficult to live in a small town where rumors and gossip are prevalent.

After his last DUI, Gilly remained clean and was helpful during their parents' later years. Because of this, Carol agreed that it made financial sense for him to stay in their parents' home, a large five-bedroom house with two efficiency apartments, while he paid down his medical bills. The second-floor apartments were rented to good-paying tenants who continued their lease after Gilly and Sophie's parents died.

Finally, everything appeared to be going well. Gilly's restaurant was gaining momentum and expanding its customer base. Carol invested her inheritance to purchase it for her brother. Even through all of the disappointment, she never lost faith in him and considered it a new start, a new chapter for him. Carol thought it was perfect, mainly because the restaurant didn't have a liquor license. She even accepted Gilly's need to drive a Corvette as a replacement for the drugs.

On Friday night, while running some errands after work, Carol decided to drive by the old homestead. There are cars stacked three deep in the driveway, with several more parked in the yard. The pulsing bass of music blasts through the open windows as she drives past, and her heart sinks. She parks down the street and walks back to the house, calculating her entry to the back door. Paul, another restaurateur and friend of Gilly's, is there, smoking a cigar, standing on the top step, taking money from a line of men waiting to go inside. Red Christmas lights are hung around the open back door. Carol marches past Paul to go inside, where her eyes scour the party goers in search of her brother. She makes the mistake of opening one bedroom door after another, shocked to find varying degrees of coupling while recognizing some of their faces from the restaurant. The last bedroom door is left partway open, allowing Carol to peek inside. There is buxom Gina with a full head of red hair, "Gina, where is Gilly?" Carol demands.

"He left about twenty minutes ago, honey. Said he had to drive some of the girls down to the motel. You can come in if you want to play." Carol slams the door in disgust, deciding she'll wait across the hall in their dad's old office for Gilly to return. Carol tries the door to the office, but it is locked. She remembers her father kept a spare key hung by a nail on the wall of the stairway leading to the basement. Surely, no one would be going down there. Unnoticed, Carol grabs the key and lets herself into the office, locking the door behind her. She surveys the room to find stacks of elegant gift boxes containing luxurious bottles of perfume paired with bathrobes, beautiful imported handbags, designer sunglasses, and silk scarves. Collapsing into her dad's old desk chair, she reads over Gilly's notes and ledger. He is using the restaurant as a guise to hire young women, and then he and Paul lure them to become prostitutes by offering them luxurious gifts and more money. Lots of money. It was all there, right in front of her; Gilly's running a brothel.

Carol didn't know it was possible to feel saddened, humiliated, and enraged simultaneously. She doesn't want to have anything to do with whatever is happening on the other side of the door, but Gilly has left her no choice. The deed to the house is in Carol's name. It's her safety net once she retires. She has to kick her brother out. But tonight, she has to put a stop to what is happening in her home. She ventures into each and every room, begging everyone to leave.

Carol calls her boss, Graham Burkes, for advice. Graham has some pull in the community and can prevent the police from showing up until she can have the locks changed on the house in the morning. Not wanting to jeopardize their professional relationship, Carol tells Graham it's a party. Nothing more.

Paul figures Carol will call the cops and is the first to hightail it out of there. Everyone else gathers their clothes and belongings, being sure to finish or take the remaining bottles of booze on their way out the door. Watching the last carload of partygoers leave feels like an eternity to her.

Carol doesn't bother to shut the lights off at 3 a.m. when she grows tired of waiting for Gilly and decides to go back to her place. She knows it will be the last time she'll leave the lights on for her brother.

The locksmith meets Carol on Saturday morning, and Gilly is nowhere to be found. It appears he didn't come home as the lights are still on. Disheartened again, she packs some of his personal items and clothes in a couple of old suitcases she found in the basement and sets them on the porch while the locks are being changed. Not wanting to face the clean-up, Carol sits down outside, noticing the contrast of the clear blue sky compared to the heavy disappointment she's feeling.

"You're all set. Looks like there was quite a party here." Says Max, the locksmith. "I always liked Gilly. He was a year ahead of me in school. It's funny how you live in a small town, but once you graduate, you rarely see your classmates." Max stood, jingling the new keys in his hand, waiting for Carol to acknowledge his presence. After a minute or two of awkward silence, he reaches down to hand Carol the keys, "I guess some of us grow up and some don't. I'll be on my way. Alright, if I have the office send you the bill?"

"That's fine, thank you," Carol responds in a whisper.

By the time Carol arrives at the office, an arc is etched into her windshield, and there's a sinking feeling in her stomach. Reminding her of the times she could sense when her brother was in trouble. Gilly hasn't made any attempt to contact her. In fact, she wonders if he's ever made it back to the house? She unlocks the front door of the law office and notices a black SUV is parked out front. The parking lights and windshield wipers are on, and a man is sitting inside sipping on a cup of what she presumes to be coffee.

It's not too long after the rain stops when Carol looks up to hear him announce his entrance, "Hello, I'm Agent Puckett." Carol's phone begins ringing with Gilly's name on her screen. She quickly turns it over and silences the call. "What can I do for you, Mr. Puckett?"

"Ms. Owens, I believe you already know why I'm here. You were given the opportunity last week with one of our agents to tell us what you knew about Gilly. Ms. Carol Owens, you are being charged with obstruction of justice for withholding information from a federal officer." Puckett handcuffs Carol and reads her rights.

Graham Burkes enters the reception area with pastries for him and Carol and is mortified to see that she's been placed in handcuffs. "What's happening?"

"Sir, I'm sorry to inform you that Ms. Owens will no longer be available to work. You know I cannot expound on the details of this matter." And with that, Puckett leads her outside, placing her in the backseat of his unmarked SUV.

Carol is trembling. *Who tipped Puckett?*

45

WILLA

Classes are coming to an end for Willa, and a new chapter in life is about to begin. The uncertainty of what the future will bring causes her to hold onto me as tightly as she ever has. The sea breeze sweeps through the cottage, and as much as she wants to go sailing with Tilghman, she's steered his invitation off twice. She wonders what will come of the information she's provided to Agent Puckett. Needing comfort, Willa goes to the bakery to pick up a cup of her favorite tea and the latest copy of the newspaper.

Leaving the bakery, she notices a "Closed" sign on the law office across the street and thinks it is odd since it is nearly noon. She hurries home to her refuge to read the news. The headline reads, Local Business Owners Charged with Trafficking. Willa goes on to read that Paul Blanchard and Gilly Owens, along with several community members, have been arrested on multiple counts, including trafficking, money laundering, sale of illegal drugs, and tax evasion. While relieved to find there is no mention of Tilghman Burkes in the article, she never imagined this idyllic town could host such atrocities. It saddens Willa to lose her innocence, to learn about the real world. Taking her last sip of tea, there's a knock at the door. Who could it be? Willa answers to find a florist delivering a stunning bouquet of fresh irises.

"Ms. Jessop?" the florist asked, confirming the address.

"That's me."

"These are for you."

"WOW, they are beautiful, thank you."

This is the first bouquet Willa has ever received. She notices the pretty botanical print paper they're wrapped in as she unties the yellow silk ribbon. Eager to find out who sent them, Willa reads the note card. *Willa, I have some exciting news to share with you. I hope you won't ask for another rain check. Please join me for pizza on the Sun Dog tonight at 6 p.m. —Hugs, Tilghman*

Willa is smitten to receive the flowers and the timing is perfect. With lifted spirits, she arranges the irises in the vase from Sophie and bounces around the cottage trying on clothes for the right outfit to wear tonight. She's listening to her favorite playlist in anticipation of seeing Tilghman.

Tilghman takes extra care to tidy the boat and keeps himself busy while he anxiously waits to see if Willa shows up. It's almost six o'clock when he steps out of the cabin in a fresh shirt to see Willa standing on the dock; she takes his breath away.

"You look beautiful."

"Why, thank you." Willa flushes from his compliment. "Permission to come aboard?"

"You bet. I was really hoping you would accept my invitation. Did I lure you with pizza?" Tilghman laughs.

"It may have been the flowers," she smiles as he takes her hand to guide her onto the boat.

"How have you been?"

"I've been busy but good. You remember what it's like when you're about to graduate and trying to finalize all of the requirements. Plus, it's been busy at the hardware store so Avery has increased my hours. I'm not complaining, I can use the money!"

"That's what I want to talk with you about." Tilghman tells her.

"Oh?"

"I was talking with my dad about you, and he suggested you stop by the office to meet him. He has an editor friend who is looking for a writer and thinks you may be a good fit. It's for a well-known quarterly publication that's privately owned."

"That sounds intriguing. I saw the office was closed today when I stopped at the Bakery. Is your father away right now?"

"No, we're still working. Unfortunately, we don't have anyone to cover the front office."

"What about Carol?"

"Haven't you heard the news? Gilly is Carol's wayward brother, and apparently, she withheld information about him from the Feds. She's been arrested and no longer works for us."

"I read the news article, but they didn't list the names of the other people involved."

"It's pretty bad. Carol's worked for Dad for twenty-seven years. I've always thought she was a little rough around the edges, but Dad insisted on keeping her. The news of her involvement really shook him up. He's tasked me with hiring her replacement, which is fair since he plans to retire eventually. It's going to be a challenge to find the right person."

"Don't you mean it's going to be an opportunity?" Willa asks, feeling a sense of relief to know Carol is gone.

"That's one of the things I like about you. You look for the positive," he says, handing her another slice of pizza.

That evening, they talk for hours as Tilghman asks Willa about her life. Listening intently to learn more about her solidified his feelings. He's falling for her and knows it, as he places his hand on hers. Willa turns his hand over and slowly traces the tattoo on his wrist.

"Thank you for inviting me for pizza," she says as they sit face-to-face. Tilghman squeezes her hand and pulls her closer. The cabin lights cast a warm glow onto the deck where they are sitting. The water twinkles with lights from nearby boats, creating an enchanting scene. Aside from a few kisses in high school, Willa has never felt like this before and can't imagine a better first date.

"No more rainchecks," he says when their lips meet, exchanging a desire that's growing. A foghorn sounds nearby, startling Willa and interrupting their kiss.

"I think that's our sign. I should probably get going, but I would like to join you for pizza again." Willa says, grabbing her sweater.

"Tomorrow?" Tilghman laughs and reaches for Willa. Hand in hand, they walk down the dock to Willa's car and exchange another long, embracing kiss. "I'll call you," Tilghman says, tapping his hands on her car door. Willa blows him a kiss as she drives away.

Watching dolphins and sincerely hoping to move through my day as gracefully as they do.

—*My Embrace*, by Lori Joseph

46

WILLA

Hi Sophie, this is Willa."

"How are you?"

"I'm doing great. I wanted to run something by you and Robert if it's possible."

"Sure. What's happening?"

"Do you remember me mentioning Tilghman, the guy who sailed by my place while you were visiting?"

"I do. In fact, he's the one you were quite taken by," Sophie responds.

Willa giggles, "Apparently, Tilghman spoke with his father about me, and he has an editor friend who is looking for a writer to join their staff. The editor requested a copy of my resume."

"That sounds promising."

"I'm excited about this opportunity and would like for you and Robert to look over my resume and give me some pointers before I submit my application."

"I'd be happy to, and I'm sure Robert will be flattered you're asking for his help. He thinks so highly of you."

"May I send it to you via email? I'll need Robert's email address, too."

"Sure and I'll forward his email to you right now."

"Thank you, Sophie. I appreciate your time. How are you doing since your visit with me?"

"I've been making great strides since our visit. Willa, you have to know you'll be an asset no matter where you land. You may have our lucky charm, but everything you need is within you. Once they meet with you, I'm sure you'll knock the interview out of the park."

"You are good for my soul." Willa replied with sincerity.

"I'll let Robert know to be watching for your email. You've got this."

"Thanks. I've gotta run. Avery is expecting me at the hardware this morning."

"Goodbye."

"Bye-bye,"

Sophie calls Robert. "Hello, Robert."

"Good morning, Sophie; what can I do for you?"

"I received a call from Willa Jessop, and she's excited to be a candidate for a potential position with a magazine. She has requested our help reviewing her resume and application and to provide her with any tips or suggestions. I've already volunteered you, I hope that's okay?"

"I'm honored. Do you know which publication it is?"

"She didn't give me the name but said it was a prestigious quarterly publication. Somebody, her lawyer friend, has a connection with the editor. She's emailing you a copy."

"I'll be watching for it."

"Very well then, enjoy your day."

"You too."

Robert opens the email from Willa and reflects on their discussions while she attended the Colony. If only he were forty years younger, she would've been someone he'd like to get to know much better. He opens the documents to find her resume reads just fine, given her age. The cover letter reveals Willa's applying to the *P. Corundum Review*. Robert leans back in his chair, contemplating whether to tell Willa that he was a contributing writer to that magazine for many years.

47

SEA GLASS

I marvel at life's tapestry, of how just one connection can lead to the next and the next. The mutual respect Sophie and Robert have for one another, as with Willa, is laudable. After Willa receives their comments, she makes a few minor adjustments to her resume and submits her application with great anticipation. Sophie's right. Everything Willa needs is within her. She is a light in this world and doesn't fully realize the impact she will have with her immeasurable perseverance and integrity.

48

SOPHIE

The long New England winter gives Sophie time to write in the evenings after work. Surrounded by artists daily, Sophie is motivated to organize her thoughts and visions to create a cohesive story. Although she's never written a book, she reads and studies the works of inspiring authors to guide her through the process. There are times when she wonders whose voice is really on the page.

Once the first few chapters were completed, writing became easier for Sophie. Whenever she needs a break from writing, she reviews voice techniques on YouTube and practices with a freshly written paragraph. Sophie does this to push herself out of her comfort zone, like she did when she accepted Hans Bauman's invitation to join him for dinner and listen to music afterwards. He was her first date since Eric.

Hans was as charming and handsome in person as Sophie had imagined him to be when talking with him on the phone. Before she knew it, they were paying each other a compliment or sharing a sandwich. Sophie found his need to hold her hand while relaying a story endearing. Originally from Germany, he told her that his lifelong love of music began when he was a youngster, learning to play the piano and the accordion. His family relocated to Switzerland, where he eventually became an engineer, patenting numerous industrial inventions that are now used internationally. Sophie was surprised when he showed genuine interest in her stories. Conversations were so invigorating and effortless that they began to chat about the possibility of Sophie accompanying him on an upcoming Mediterranean cruise. The young girl inside her wanted to jump at the invitation, but the rational woman she'd become suggested things might be moving a little too fast. Sensing her hesitance, Hans says, "I completely understand if now is not convenient. You can let me know, and we will plan for another time."

Sophie shares the first few chapters of her manuscript with Hans, and his encouragement means the world to Sophie, giving her the courage to finish her story.

Although his time at the Colony is far too brief, his candor and insight were remarkable and heartfelt to Sophie.

As a thank you for arranging his stay in the woods next to the water in the O'Keefe Cabin, Hans gifted her a small plaque. It reads, "Waldeinsamkeit, which he explains, is the joyful feeling of solitude or the spiritual connection one feels when they are in the woods." Hans goes on to say, "It's much the same way I feel when we're together," embracing Sophie for one more hug and whispering, "till next time," before leaving to continue his travels.

Time passed, and recurring thoughts of Hans came to Sophie's mind. She made a vow to herself not to be the first to call, yet she wondered why she hadn't heard from him. The timing of his visit to the Colony was in some way mysterious because it provided the push or validation she needed to continue with her manuscript.

In the final chapter of her book, Sophie writes: It was barely a brush of their hands to exchange the mistaken luggage when Claudette felt a zing travel through her body. She couldn't shake the notion that she and this fellow traveler were once lovers in a previous lifetime.

Sophie knows she is more than a conduit to write this story. The details and events that took place in her dreams imbued her being. With this newfound awareness, she let go of the dis-ease she held onto from Eric's betrayal. Sophie understood there was no benefit in harboring those feelings any longer.

Early the following morning, after much consideration, she called Eric to say, "I want you to know it's taken me a long time, but I don't hate you anymore. I don't like the lifestyle you've chosen, but I am willing to accept it. I want our children, and hopefully grandchildren, to have a relationship with us. It's important to me that they know they came from a place of love. However it looks, it was love."

"Sophie, I never stopped loving you. I know you may find that hard to believe, but I really do love you. I want our kids to know this, too," Eric said, weeping. "I'm so glad you finally called."

The culmination of making peace with Eric and finishing the manuscript was monumental for Sophie. She put on her boots and went to work with a copy of her story in hand.

"Good morning, Robert."

"I thought it was you. I heard you coming in those boots." Robert smiles.

"You know how much I respect you. I was wondering if you would be willing to read my manuscript?"

"Sure. I'd be happy too. When do you need it back?"

"Does a week or two work for your schedule?"

"That's doable," Robert replies, fanning the pages. "I look forward to reading *Passage*."

Robert completes the book in four days, making a few minor edits.

"Sophie, you've written a unique and beautiful story. I believe you have a good chance of getting this published. I wish you luck."

"You're too kind. I can always count on you to make my day. What are you working on there?"

Robert brushes some wood shavings aside, "I have a little time between classes to add a few editorial notches to my walking stick."

"Looks like you're running out of room. You're gonna need another stick."

"I'm running out of time, too," Robert says jokingly.

"You're going to outlive all of us. I'd put money on it! Now, I'm off to make the changes you recommended. I really appreciate you," Sophie says, leaving his office.

No news is good news. That's what Sophie kept telling herself as she submitted her work to numerous publishers week after week. Several months passed before Sophie received a call from an unknown number. Letting the call go to voicemail, she expected the caller to hang up. Much to her surprise, they left a message.

"Hello, this is Reginald Lang. I'm calling to congratulate you. Shelbourne Publishing would like to extend an offer to you for Passage. I'll send you the details and contract via email. We look forward to working with you."

Sophie must have replayed the message 20 times before calling her family and friends with the good news.

Completing the novella gave Sophie the freedom to dream and imagine her life going forward. And with the help of Agent Lang, Sophie's introduction into the literary world was catapulted. She envisioned hosting the book launch wearing the stunning necklace donated by Elizabeth McKenzie for the Gala's Live Auction last summer. Sophie was the highest bidder and won the necklace. She loved how it showcased her eyes and the line of her neck.

Sophie decided to host her own private book launch celebration in California's Wine Country, where she once traveled to for the Colony. The Gardetto Estate was constructed with heavy stones and pillars, featuring ornate iron hinges on the shutters around the arched windows and oversized doors that opened onto the patio. On the veranda, there were pots with flowers cascading to the ground and trees strung with white lights. The thirty-foot rustic table made from the timber cleared to build the barn sat waiting for guests, and now Sophie was going to share this magnificent property with all of her dearest friends.

It is September, and the winds sweep across the vineyards ripe with olives and grapes. Sophie arrives mid-afternoon, a day in advance of the celebration, to find the most exquisite bouquet waiting for her upon check-in. They are so extraordinary that she can't imagine who would've sent them. The desk clerk says they were delivered just before her arrival, but there is no note attached to them.

"Who was the florist?" Sophie asks, so she can contact them to properly thank her admirer.

The clerk tells her, "They were delivered by a gentleman driving a white Land Rover. There wasn't any indication on the vehicle that it was from a floral shop."

How unfortunate she hadn't arrived just a few minutes earlier, so that she could've solved the mystery.

Thinking that someone may remark about them and give her a lead on who sent them, she says, "May I ask you to set the flowers on the table outside so everyone can enjoy them?"

Michael, the charismatic owner of the estate, makes her feel like she's an old friend. His appearance reminds her of the famous chef Paul Prudhomme. "After you get settled, you may find it inviting to sit over at the lookout. It's a short walk to the right from the patio. I'll send over a glass of wine and have Jana put together something for you to nibble on."

"Thank you, that sounds lovely. I will take you up on the suggestion."

The entrance to the overlook is flanked by crimson roses, creating a canopy to walk under. The sound of the pebble-stone path beneath her feet evokes a memory from Sophie's youth; the days when she rode her bike down the gravel lane to pick ripened berries. The view from the overlook is stunning—acres upon acres of rolling vineyards are bathed in the late afternoon sunlight.

Enveloped by her surroundings and good fortune, Sophie sits, sipping her wine, reflecting on how she's arrived in such a place and the paths that led her to this occasion. She's proud of her accomplishments yet still wonders if her guests will find her book worthy of celebration. They are flying across the country to attend her reading, taking time away from their families and using precious vacation time to be with her. She hopes they won't be disappointed. Watching the sun slip behind the hills, she returns to the lodge to prepare her notes. Although her debut reading is with close friends, she wants to be able to answer their questions. Quite honestly, she wants to do so with eloquence. Such consideration will prepare her for future readings where the readers might not be so forgiving.

Her nerves, now softened from the wine, allow her to focus on the questionnaire. She paces the floor, reading the questions and then answering them in front of the mirror. Nearly finished, she looks at herself rather than listening. There, in the mirror, is a middle-aged woman with graying hair and slightly slumped shoulders answering questions with intimate detail. Dressed in black and white, she notices her eyes are not conveying the words she is speaking. Adjusting her posture, she confidently answers the remaining questions with a sparkle in her eyes. Much better. Feeling content from rehearsing, Sophie decides to take a late-night stroll when she hears Michael call out,

"Come join me, next to the fire. So how was your day?" he asked while pouring her a glass of wine.

"Pinch me, I still can't believe I'm here."

"We're delighted you've chosen to be here."

While sitting under the stars, Sophie learns that Michael built the estate with a dream in mind. It was truly a labor of love, and now he enjoys sharing his dream. The two of them sit by the fire sharing stories as if they've known each other for years. When the last log burned down to embers, it was time to call it a night. On the way inside, Sophie stopped by the table to smell the flowers.

"You must have a special admirer to send you such a beautiful bouquet!"

"I agree with you. I have no idea who sent the flowers, but they're exceptional. Goodnight, and thank you for a lovely evening."

"The pleasure is mine. Goodnight."

The following morning, Sophie awakens, slowly taking in the room's luxurious decor from her comfy bed. The floor-to-ceiling arched windows allow for a cross breeze of fresh air scented with roses and rosemary. The antique writing desk and light fixtures appear to be imported. To be pampered, she treats herself to a morning at the spa, complete with a facial, massage, manicure, and pedicure. She times it perfectly as guests will be arriving early in the afternoon, with the event officially starting with cocktails and hors d'oeuvres at 5 p.m.

The veranda is a sight beyond belief. Sophie's guests are all decked out for the occasion and buzzing with excitement. Michael honors Sophie's request to have music playing in the background while everyone takes in the view and is in awe of the estate.

"Liddy!" Sophie shouts and hurries over to hug her dear friend. "It's so good to see you."

"I am so proud of you. Sophie, you did it. You wrote a book!" Liddy said, hugging her dearest friend.

"It's been a long time coming, and it's finally here," Sophie responds with teary eyes.

"You can't start crying now, everybody's here." Liddy laughs and changes the subject. "This is quite the place. How did you find it?"

"The Colony hosted a small event here for our West Coast Benefactors and Artists. Let me introduce you to Darla and Marc. Darla and I met at a painting class. Darla sends me inspirational messages and encouragement. Her husband, Marc, and I became friends while attending many soccer games to watch our kids play.

"Darla and Marc, this is my dear friend, Liddy. She and I live in New England and have been good friends for many years. I'll let you get acquainted so I can go and greet the others."

Sophie turns and is astonished to see Willa standing there, waiting to congratulate her. "I can't believe you made the trip. I am so very glad you came."

"I wouldn't miss it for the world." Willa responds, pressing the sea glass into Sophie's hand. "I thought it might be useful for you to borrow it for your debut." Willa winks and clinks her glass to Sophie's.

And on it went until Sophie made all of the introductions.

"May I propose a toast?" Sophie says, "Lift your glasses and take in the night. I am so grateful for the support and friendship you have given me. It is with highest regard that I welcome you and promise that I could not have done it without each of you. I love you. Salute!"

Placed down the center of the table on either side of the flowers are copies of her newly released book, *Passage*. The setting is magical as they share dinner and laughs, catching up on the latest happenings.

Michael turns the music down as dessert is being served when Sophie tings her glass with a spoon to announce, "I'm going to read to you while you enjoy dessert. As many of you know, this story has come to me through visions or dreams. The setting is 1836 in the small French village of Montrol-Sénard."

"Many months have passed since François' death, and poor Claudette is floundering. The silence in their modest home is deafening. Heartbroken, she feels as though she has no purpose. There are no family members left in their homeland, and their lifelong dream to go to America is just that, a dream. Claudette remembers the letters François sent to her before they were married. Telling her of the life they could one day have in America. The letters are filled with such hope, such love, but they could never save enough to afford the travel. Claudette goes to the closet to retrieve the satchel, a wedding gift from her mother, who had arthritic hands and stitched it for her. She has kept François' letters in there for safekeeping and begins reading each letter by candlelight night after night. Thinking it will somehow bring him back. For their last anniversary, François gave her a beautiful little bottle of perfume that she cherishes. She dabs a tiny bit of the fragrance into her hair, reserving this luxury for special occasions. She is saddened to think there will be no more occasions, gifts of perfume, and no more of François' tenderness. Only the memories they have shared.

As Claudette packs up his clothes to give to charity, she finds a newspaper clipping tucked into his worn woolen jacket. It is the schedule for the Blue Royal, a ship that transports passengers and cargo to America, and she knows she has to go. At the age of eighty-one, she sells their home and belongings and sets off for America to honor her late husband's wish."

When finished, Sophie looks up to see there was never any reason to be nervous. Everyone applauds and surrounds her with hugs and affection. The wine flows with the Q&A, and Sophie has done well to prepare. As the evening is winding down, she asks, "Who should I thank for these flowers?" Nobody could offer any information, but this led to an entirely inappropriate round of speculation, accompanied by jokes and laughter, as the evening came to a close. "What a wonderful night we've shared! Reading to my friends and answering their questions, has given me the confidence to begin my book tour."

Sunday morning came too quickly as her guests were reluctant to leave such a beautiful place. The front desk clerk arranged for a car service to take Sophie to the airport at 1:15, allowing her to see them off.

Sophie walks with Michael to the overlook, taking in one last view of the estate, and says, "I want to thank you for such a memorable experience."

"You must be quite a lady to have friends travel so far to share your success. I think I will have to read it too! He smiles. Handing her a copy to autograph. "Maybe next time you can plan to stay a few more days?"

Sophie chuckles, "I would love for there to be a next time ...but let's see how I do with this first book."

The gravel lane announces the arrival of a car. Michael sees a white Land Rover with tinted windows pull next to the lodge.

"Sophie, please excuse me, I will go check to see who this is and be right back."

Michael meets and escorts the driver to the foyer where Sophie's luggage is stowed. They chat and Michael agrees to give him a couple of minutes to load her luggage before walking Sophie to the car.

Returning to the overlook, Michael stands next to Sophie in quiet appreciation. "It has been very nice to have you as our guest. I'm afraid to say, it's time to go. Your ride is waiting. Shall I walk you to your car?" "

"How does it get any better than this?" Sophie asks as Michael offers his arm.

They walked under the canopy of roses before Sophie looked up to see a familiar face standing next to the Range Rover. "Hans Bauman! How did you know...and the flowers?"

They hug each other as if never to let go.

Michael takes his cue and steps away to answer his phone.

Grinning, Hans tells her, "I respectfully did not want to interrupt your focus on your writing because I did not want to be responsible for you not finishing your book. You see, I have been waiting patiently to pick up where we left off. Now, if you are willing? Let's take a drive to celebrate before your book tour.

49

SEA GLASS

Willa accepted the opportunity to become a full-time associate for the P. Corundum Review and waited till the end of her shift at the hardware store to tell her boss. Although selfishly disappointed, Avery understands and says, “Willa, if you ever need some additional money, you are welcome to come back.” But in her heart, Avery knows it’s a long shot and goes on to say, “I wish nothing but the best for you,” stepping around her desk to give Willa a hug goodbye.

“I really appreciate the offer, Avery. It means a lot to me.”

“I probably went overboard singing your praise when they called me for a reference,” and they both laughed.

“I’m sure I’ll be stopping in from time to time for my DIY projects. It’s been great to work for you. Thanks again.”

Willa’s phone rings as she is walking out the door.

“Tilghman, did you know you have an innate sense of when to reach out to me? How are you?”

“I’m good, I was calling to see how Avery took the news?”

“She’s sad to see me leave, but did admit she gave me a great referral.”

“How about I pick you up around 7 o’clock and take you to dinner to celebrate the start of your new career?”

“Sounds great. See you soon.”

On their way to the restaurant, Tilghman asks, “How do you feel about making a quick stop at the country club on our way to dinner?”

“That’s fine. I’ve never been to a country club. Am I dressed appropriately?”

“You look amazing. My parents are having drinks with some friends in the clubhouse, and I thought you might want to share your good news with them.”

"I'd love to. I intended to send your dad a personal thank you for the connection, but thanking him in person is even better."

"I'm sure they'll both be happy for you."

Tilghman and Willa enter the clubhouse, and all eyes fell on them. Willa tries her best to pretend she doesn't notice. Thankfully, Tilghman quickly maneuvers them through the crowd to the high-top table where his parents are sitting with friends.

"First things first," Tilghman says and winks at Willa. "Mom, I'd like you to meet Willa Jessop."

"Mrs. Burkes, it is so nice to meet you," Willa says, trying her best not to fidget.

"Olivia. Call me Olivia," she says, admiring Willa. "Willa Jessop, you are radiant in sapphire blue. I just love your dress. I can see why Tilghman is quite taken by you."

"Now, honey, let's not embarrass Willa in front of our friends." Graham Burkes says, looking directly at Willa. "Rumor has it you have something to tell us?"

"Yes. It's good to see you again, Mr. Burkes."

"Please, call me Graham."

Tilghman nudges Willa to speak. "I was offered and accepted the position at *P. Corundum Review*. I start work on Monday."

"Hey, that's terrific news. Congratulations."

"Graham, I owe it to you for helping me make the connection. I'm sincerely grateful."

"Nonsense. All I did was give you a name. You're the one who made it happen."

Tilghman puts his arm around Willa, giving her a squeeze.

"Will you be joining us for dinner?" Graham asks.

"Not tonight. We just wanted to swing by and share the good news." Tilghman replies.

"Fantastic. We're glad you did."

"See you later." Both Tilghman and Willa say in unison, recognizing their simpatico.

"Graham leans over and whispers in Olivia's ear, "I believe our son has found a keeper."

Months into her position at the magazine, Willa is writing a story based on Carl Jung's belief in the interconnectedness of the collective unconscious.

"How's the story coming along?" asks James, her senior colleague.

Willa stops what she is doing and asks, "James, do you believe there are no coincidences?" She studies James while he considers a thoughtful response to her question. James has a reputation for being an alchemist with words, cultivating dynamic stories worth printing. She hopes his response will trigger just the right thought for her to complete her story on time.

"Willa, if I were to state my belief, you will not be writing from what you know, but rather from a place you think you know. Come with me."

She follows him down the hallway through a door past his office. Three floors down, the stairway leads them to a room she didn't know existed. "This room contains P. Corundum's overflow of archives," James tells her as he turns on the lights. There are thousands of hours of research stored in this room. Take a look around. You're bound to find what you're searching for in here."

"Thank you for showing me this gold mine," says Willa, astounded by the sheer volume of information before her.

"Happy to help. I need to get back upstairs for a meeting. Please shut the lights off when you leave."

During her research, Willa discovers an in-depth file on the topic buried in the archives. Trembling with excitement, she delves through the folders to find someone has already done extensive research, including information about the philosopher's stone theory and spiritual transformation. While scouring the pages, something catches her eye, so she begins checking the next several folders to find that the research completed was signed by R. Newton.

This discovery leads her to consider the interconnectedness of her own relationships and how each and every one of them contributes to the woman she's become. Meeting Robert and Sophie was no coincidence. Nor was her discovery of Sea Glass. She can feel it in her bones and will use this knowledge as fuel to complete the article.

Willa has learned that feeling resistance to anything is the body's way of communicating. The more we resist a situation or an idea, the more complicated it can get. Repeating itself. But when we allow and accept these circumstances to flow through us and decide we'd rather choose to feel better, like Sophie did, that awareness affords us the ability to live our truth. It is with this understanding that Willa settles in to write her story of connectivity and the power of Sea Glass.

When the article was published, Willa sent Robert a package from *P. Corundum Review*. Enclosed was the latest copy of the magazine, along with a compensation check and a letter stating that he had received editorial credit for his extensive research. Robert remembers the day his article was tabled. The sudden attacks on September 11, 2001, put the country in a tailspin, causing everyone to shift their focus, including the magazine's editor.

Receiving the thoughtful letter from Willa Jessop was a boost to his soul. Robert is proud that he hasn't lost his touch, his knack for recognizing talent. He tucks Willa's personal note of sentiment into his shirt pocket, keeping it close to his heart.

With Enlightened Acknowledgment

Sea Glass would not have been possible without the love and support from those who have provided me with the necessary feedback and encouragement to write this story. I am eternally grateful to those who have endured countless conversations and edits so that I could find my voice. Our kinship means the world to me as you have lifted me in numerous ways to grow as a friend and writer. I am astounded to have connected with all of you for many reasons beyond writing this book.

Special thanks to my beta readers, Valerie DeMarines, Kristin Ging, Sarah Johnson, Dorothy Leach, Leda LeBlance, Betty Malicoat, Rich Mills, Megan Moore, Elizabeth Sikierski, and Dot Valhauli, for your time and courteous feedback. Your light shines within these pages.

As with any project, there is a foundation to build upon, and I am sincerely grateful to these individuals for lending their expertise. Writer Judy Burch provided invaluable insight and guided me through a master class of grammatical refinement. With forged tears, I knew I had her blessing to keep writing. Trilogy Author Kaye Harrison lent me her essential editing prowess to ensure the story's clarity and flow. Until the publication of Connectivity Through the Ages, I had never heard of author Stephen Newton. His review of that book has led me to his prolific and profound writing talent that he has willingly shared. Always encouraging, I am so fortunate to be guided by his wisdom and friendship.

I owe sincere gratitude to my supportive family and my husband, Tim. With your willingness and patience, you have gifted me ample time to write. While I was home writing the final chapters, Tim was traveling in Scotland. It was no coincidence that he stumbled upon a piece of sea glass on the shore of Loch Morie. Further validating my heartfelt belief that there is an energy connecting everybody and everything in this world for a greater purpose we cannot see.

About the Author

LORI JOSEPH—poet, author, and eternal optimist whose work explores connection, resilience, and moments of joy found in everyday life.

Sea Glass is her first novella. For more information about Lori and her work, visit www.lorijoseph.com

www.ingramcontent.com/pod-product-compliance
Lightning Source LLC
LaVergne TN
LVHW090523110826
845146LV00003B/956

* 9 7 9 8 9 9 4 9 7 9 5 0 1 *